The Alpha Mayor

A Protective Alpha Fated Mates Steamy Age Gap Omegaverse Romance

Ash Jade

D ear Reader,

Welcome to *Rescued by the Rider.*

This is an omegaverse romance—a version of the world where people have secondary dynamics (alpha, beta, omega) that affect scent, pheromones, and instinct. In this story, those instincts can be loud, but they don't get to make decisions for anyone. What matters here is choice: communication, consent, and the steady, hard-earned work of building trust.

A few things to know before you begin:

This book includes material that may be difficult for some readers. I keep a detailed, up-to-date list of content warnings on my website (so you can check what you need without spoilers):

https://www.ashjadeauthor.com/pages/content-warnings

Intimate scenes are explicit and consent-centered. Every touch is asked for, every boundary honored. And while the road is steep, this is still a romance with a guaranteed HEA.

If you're ready for a protective alpha who earns it, an omega who refuses to be owned, and a love built on choice instead of instinct, turn the page.

— Ash Jade

Contents

1

—·—

I grip the steering wheel of my ancient Honda, knuckles white against the peeling leather as the "Welcome to Sanctuary" sign appears around the bend. My scent blockers are fresh, my suppressants are holding, and the town sprawls before me like some fairytale mirage after six hours of mountain roads. This is it. The place where omegas come to disappear, to breathe, to start over. The place where I'm going to become someone new.

Pine trees give way to quaint storefronts as I ease into town. Main Street looks ripped from a greeting card—family-owned shops with hand-painted signs, hanging flower baskets swinging in the mountain breeze, a courthouse with an actual clock tower. It's almost too perfect, almost suspicious in its welcoming charm.

"Please be real," I whisper to no one.

My old pack would laugh themselves sick seeing me here. Little Lila Morgan, the omega who couldn't hack it in the real world, running to some backwoods sanctuary town. But they're not here. Nobody from before is here. That's the whole fucking point.

I follow the directions from my rental agreement to a small apartment complex on Aspen Lane. It's modest but clean—weathered brick, small balconies, nothing fancy. Just what I need. Just what I can afford on an intern's salary at the town council.

The key sticks in the lock, requiring a specific jiggle-and-thrust that I'll need to perfect. Inside, the apartment smells of lemon cleaner and fresh paint. One bedroom, one bath, a kitchenette, and a living space that could generously be called "cozy." The furniture is sparse but functional—a futon couch, coffee table, small dining set, and a bed I can see through the bedroom doorway.

I haul in my two suitcases and backpack—my entire life condensed to what fits in a Honda Civic. No alpha's scent lingers on my clothes or skin. No pack bonds tug at my chest. Just me, starting over at twenty-two with a political science degree and desperation disguised as ambition.

"Home sweet home," I mutter, dropping my bags. The sound echoes slightly in the empty space. I should unpack, but my stomach growls, reminding me I haven't eaten since that gas station burrito four hours ago. Food first, then settling in.

Back outside, the late afternoon sun casts long shadows across the street. The mountain air feels cleaner than anything I've breathed before, sharp with pine and something wild that makes my omega senses perk up. I follow my nose and the rumble in my stomach down Main Street, taking in the details I missed during my drive in.

A hardware store with rocking chairs lined up outside. A bookshop with a sleepy cat in the window. A sheriff's office where a deputy raises a hand in casual greeting as I pass. Everyone moves with unhurried purpose, and several people nod hello without the usual omega assessment I'm used to—no obvious scenting, no dominance posturing.

The diner sits at the corner of Main and Pine, its neon "Marge's Place" sign humming in the dusk. Large windows reveal checkered floors and red vinyl booths. The bell jingles as I push open the door, and the warm air hits me—coffee, grease, pie, and the mingled scents of at least a dozen people.

Conversations dip briefly as heads turn toward me, then resume at a slightly higher volume. I feel the weight of curious glances as I slide into an empty booth by the window. The plastic menu is sticky at the edges, featuring comfort food classics and daily specials scrawled in marker on a whiteboard behind the counter.

"Well now, you must be our new intern."

I look up to find a woman in her sixties standing beside my table, coffeepot in one hand, order pad in the other. Her gray hair is pulled into a no-nonsense bun, and her eyes are sharp but kind. Her scent is neutral—a beta—with notes of coffee and something floral.

"News travels fast," I say, surprised.

She laughs, deep and genuine. "Honey, this is Sanctuary. We practically knew you were coming before you did. I'm Marge." She fills the mug in front of me without asking. "Owner, cook, and unofficial town crier. You're Lila Morgan from Eastern State University, starting Monday at Town Hall."

I blink. "That's... both impressive and slightly terrifying."

"Small towns." Marge shrugs, unapologetic. "We don't get many newcomers who stay. Most just pass through on their way to somewhere else." Her eyes narrow, assessing. "But you're here to stay, aren't you?"

I take a sip of coffee to buy time. It's good—strong and not burnt like chain diners. "That's the plan."

Marge nods, satisfied. "Mayor Carrington mentioned you impressed him in your interview. Said your ideas for community outreach were 'refreshingly pragmatic.' High praise from him."

My chest warms with unexpected pride. "I didn't think he'd remember my interview. It was just over Zoom."

"Oh, Nate remembers everything." Marge taps her order pad. "Now, what can I get you? Special tonight is meatloaf, but between us, the chicken fried steak is better."

I order the chicken fried steak, and Marge disappears behind the counter, shouting my order to an unseen cook. While waiting, I observe the diner's other patrons—a family with two young children, an elderly couple sharing pie, three men in work clothes arguing good-naturedly over something in the newspaper.

Marge returns periodically to refill my coffee and drop morsels of town information like breadcrumbs. The festival planning committee needs new blood. The hardware store owner's son just had twins. Sheriff Jake and his mate Olivia run the most respected pack in the county. Mayor Carrington—Nate—is a widower who rebuilt the town after the mining company pulled out ten years ago.

"Single, too," Marge adds with a wink that makes me choke on my coffee. "Though don't get any ideas. Man's married to this town."

"I'm not looking for—" I start.

"Course you're not, honey." Marge pats my hand. "Nobody comes to Sanctuary looking for love. They come looking for safety, for peace." Her eyes soften. "Whatever you're running from, you don't have to look over your shoulder here."

The statement hits uncomfortably close to home. "I'm not running," I lie.

Marge just smiles. "Eat your food before it gets cold."

The meal is delicious, hearty, and exactly what I needed after the long drive. By the time I finish, night has fallen, and the diner has emptied except for a few stragglers. I pay my bill, leaving a generous tip that makes Marge raise an eyebrow.

"See you tomorrow," she says, not a question.

I nod. "Probably. Best food I've had in months."

The walk back to my apartment takes on a dreamlike quality. Street lamps cast pools of golden light on the sidewalk. Stars pepper the sky, more than I've ever seen in the city. For the first time in years, my shoulders relax completely. No alphas tracking my scent. No pack politics to navigate. Just me, the night air, and a town that already knows my name but doesn't seem to hold my status against me.

In my apartment, I finally unpack, hanging clothes in the empty closet, arranging toiletries in the bathroom, placing my single framed photo—me at graduation, alone but smiling—on the nightstand. Each item finding its place feels like another step toward this new life taking root.

As I curl up in my new bed, exhaustion and hope battle for dominance. Tomorrow I'll explore more, prepare for Monday, maybe even meet more locals. But tonight, I breathe deeply and let myself believe that maybe, just maybe, Sanctuary will live up to its name.

2

— · —

I arrive at Town Hall twenty minutes early, clutching my leather portfolio like it's some kind of shield. My blouse is pressed, my pencil skirt professional, my hair tamed into submission. I've doubled up on scent blockers today, slathering the clinical-smelling lotion along my pulse points until my natural omega scent is buried beneath synthetic neutrality. First impressions matter. First day jitters are normal. First time meeting the mayor in person is absolutely not making my stomach flip like I'm sixteen again.

Town Hall stands at the heart of Sanctuary—a two-story brick building with white columns and wide steps leading to heavy oak doors. Inside, the foyer smells of lemon polish and old wood, with portraits of former mayors lining the walls. A circular reception desk sits empty; apparently, Sanctuary doesn't bother with security checks.

The council chamber is upstairs, a high-ceilinged room with tall windows that flood the space with morning light. A horseshoe-shaped table dominates the center, surrounded by cushioned chairs for the council members. Public seating fills the back half—simple wooden benches that remind me of church pews.

I set up at a small desk marked "Staff" with a handwritten "Intern" sticky note slapped on for clarification. Nice. At least they remembered I was coming.

The council members begin filtering in around 8:45. A woman in her fifties with a teacher's brisk efficiency—Claire Jensen, according to the nameplate she places at her seat. An older man with silver hair and farmer's hands—Walter Reed. A younger woman with sharp eyes and a sharper suit—Samantha Doyle. Each offers me a curious nod or greeting, their scents mingling in the air—beta, beta, alpha. I memorize names, positions, making mental notes of potential allies or obstacles.

At precisely 9:00, the door at the back of the chamber opens, and something in the air changes.

I don't need to look up to know who has entered. My omega instincts snap to attention like a rubber band pulled taut. The hair on my arms rises. My pulse kicks against my throat.

Mayor Nathaniel Carrington strides into the room, and the air seems to part for him.

He's taller than he appeared on my computer screen during the interview—broad-shouldered, lean-hipped, moving with the easy confidence of an alpha who doesn't need to prove his dominance. Late thirties, maybe early forties. His dark hair is threaded with silver at the temples, and the lines around his eyes speak of both laughter and loss. He wears a charcoal suit that fits his frame perfectly, no tie, white shirt open at the collar.

But it's his scent that hits me like a physical blow.

Pine. Smoke. Mountain air. Raw, undiluted alpha. The scent blockers I applied so carefully might as well be water for all the protection they offer. Beneath the professional facade, my omega whimpers in recognition.

"Good morning, everyone." His voice is deeper in person, with a gravelly edge that scrapes pleasantly down my spine. "Let's get started."

He glances around the room, nodding at familiar faces, and then his eyes land on me. Recognition flickers, followed by something I can't name. Our gazes lock across the chamber.

One heartbeat.

Two.

Three.

Electricity arcs between us, sharp and unexpected. My skin prickles, hot then cold, a flush crawling up my neck. His nostrils flare slightly—catching my scent despite the blockers—and his pupils dilate, dark eclipsing blue. For a fraction of a second, I glimpse something primal in his expression before he masters it, his face returning to professional neutrality.

"Ms. Morgan," he says, breaking the silence. "Welcome to Sanctuary. I trust your move went smoothly?"

I clear my throat, fighting for composure. "Yes, thank you, Mayor Carrington."

"Nate," he corrects, the corner of his mouth lifting slightly. "We don't stand on ceremony here."

Nate. The informality feels intimate on my tongue, though I haven't spoken it aloud. I just nod, not trusting my voice.

He turns to the council, calling the meeting to order, and I exhale shakily. What the hell was that? I've been around plenty of alphas before. I'm not some sheltered omega who swoons at the first whiff of pheromones. But Nate's presence feels like gravity, constantly pulling at my awareness even as I stare determinedly at my notebook.

The meeting progresses with reports, votes, discussions of community issues. I take notes mechanically, trying to focus on the content rather than the man at the head of the table. But my eyes betray me, drawn to his hands as he gestures to emphasize a point, to the strong column of his throat when he throws his head back in rare laughter, to the intensity in his gaze as he considers each speaker.

His leadership style fascinates me. He listens more than he speaks, extracting opinions from each council member before offering his own. When disagreements arise, he mediates with patience and surprising humor. This isn't an alpha who rules through intimidation or brute force. His authority seems earned through respect.

"Which brings us to the Founder's Festival," Nate says, turning a page in his agenda. "We're six weeks out and still short on volunteers. Ms. Morgan, I believe you expressed interest in community events during your interview. Perhaps you'd be willing to assist the planning committee?"

All eyes turn to me. I straighten in my chair, ignoring the flutter in my stomach at being singled out. "Of course. I'd be happy to help."

"Excellent. Samantha chairs the committee—she'll get you up to speed." He holds my gaze a beat too long, and that current zips between us again. "I think you'll bring a fresh perspective."

Is it my imagination, or does his voice drop slightly on the word "fresh"? The alpha councilwoman, Samantha, glances between us with narrowed eyes, her nose twitching subtly. Scenting. My face heats under her scrutiny.

The remainder of the meeting passes in a blur of budget approvals and infrastructure discussions. I jot notes automatically while hyperaware of every shift, every breath from the head of the table. When Nate calls for adjournment, I feel like I've run a marathon, muscles tense from maintaining my composure.

Council members file out with casual goodbyes. I gather my things slowly, hoping to slip out unnoticed while Nate converses with Walter about road repairs. But as I reach the door, his voice stops me.

"Ms. Morgan—Lila."

I turn, clutching my portfolio against my chest like armor. "Yes, Mayor—Nate?"

He approaches, hands in pockets, casual yet imposing. Up close, his scent is even more potent, wrapping around me like an embrace. My inner omega purrs, recognizing something essential in him that calls to me on a cellular level.

"I wanted to personally welcome you to the team." His eyes, startlingly blue under dark brows, study my face. "Your resume was impressive, but credentials only tell part of the story. Why Sanctuary? Eastern State graduates usually head for the city."

The question is innocuous, but his expression suggests he sees more than I want to reveal. I meet his gaze, refusing to show the nervousness fluttering in my chest.

"I wanted somewhere I could make an actual difference," I say, offering the same half-truth

I've been telling everyone. "Not just be a cog in a machine."

His head tilts slightly, eyes never leaving mine. "And?"

"And what?" I ask, thrown off by his persistence.

"The rest of the reason." His voice lowers, intimate in the empty chamber. "People come to Sanctuary for new beginnings, yes, but usually because they need to leave something behind."

My pulse jumps. How does he see through me so easily? I force a casual shrug, though my grip on the portfolio tightens. "Isn't that my business?"

Rather than taking offense, a smile curves his mouth—a genuine one that softens the angles of his face and makes him look younger. "Fair enough. Your past is your own. But know that if you ever want to share it, my door is always open."

He steps back, breaking the invisible tether between us. "Samantha will email you about the festival committee. First meeting is Thursday evening."

I nod, grateful for the return to professional territory. "I'll be there."

As I walk out of Town Hall into the bright morning sunshine, his scent clings to me like a memory. I take a deep breath of clean mountain air, trying to clear my head and slow my racing heart.

Professional, Lila. Keep it professional. He's the mayor. He's at least fifteen years older. He's your boss.

But deep in my core, where instinct overrules logic, my omega has already recognized something my rational mind refuses to acknowledge: Mayor Nathaniel Carrington is dangerous to my carefully constructed plans—not because he threatens my safety, but because he threatens my solitude.

And solitude is what I came to Sanctuary to find. Isn't it?

3

Three weeks into my new job, and I've developed an obsessive relationship with spreadsheets. Founder's Festival budget projections. Vendor applications. Volunteer schedules. Anything with neat columns and clear parameters that don't smell like pine and smoke or have eyes that follow me across rooms. I've become the most productive intern in Sanctuary history, according to Claire from the council. What she doesn't know is that productivity is my only defense against the ridiculous, inappropriate attraction I feel every time Mayor Carrington walks into a room.

I tab through another vendor application, squinting at the tiny font. Outside my cubicle, the municipal office hums with afternoon activity—phones ringing, printers whirring, the coffee machine gurgling its death rattle again. I've carved out a small corner of Town Hall for myself, nestled between the records room and the water cooler—prime real estate for eavesdropping, terrible for avoiding gossip.

Which is how I learned about Nate's wife.

It was during my first week, while refilling my water bottle. Two older clerks, not realizing I was there, spoke in those hushed tones people use when they want to pretend they're not gossiping.

"—been almost five years since Rebecca passed," one said. "Man needs to move on eventually."

"Losing your mate like that... some never recover. He poured everything into rebuilding this town after the accident. Some say it's the only thing that kept him going."

"Still, thirty-eight is too young to be alone. Alpha like that needs—"

They spotted me then, conversation cutting off with guilty smiles. But I'd heard enough to piece together the outline: Widower. Tragic accident. Devoted to the town that became his lifeline.

Later, I found myself in the records room, ostensibly searching for historical festival documents, actually flipping through newspaper archives. There it was, five years back: "Mayor's Wife Killed in Mountain Accident." The photo showed a younger Nate with a beautiful dark-haired woman, both laughing at something off-camera. The happiness in his face made my chest ache.

I slammed the binder shut, ashamed of my morbid curiosity. It wasn't my business. None of it was.

Yet knowing about his loss has only made it harder to ignore him. Now I notice things I shouldn't—the careful way he maintains professional distance from everyone, the moments when memory shadows his eyes, the wedding ring no longer on his finger but the pale band of skin where it used to be.

"Ms. Morgan? Did you hear me?"

I snap back to the present, blinking up at Councilwoman Doyle—Samantha—who stands at my cubicle entrance with an expectant expression.

"Sorry, just focused on these applications." I straighten, professional smile firmly in place. "What was that?"

She sighs, impatient. "The mayor wants to see the preliminary budget report. Today."

"Of course." I nod, gathering the folder I'd prepared yesterday. Always stay one step ahead—my new mantra. "I can take it to him now."

"No need." She holds out her hand. "I'm heading that way."

Something territorial flares in my chest—ridiculous, unwanted. "Actually, I have questions about the stage setup that I should ask him directly."

Her eyebrows lift slightly, nostrils flaring in that subtle way alphas have when they're scenting for deception. "Fine. He's in his office."

I slip past her, folder clutched to my chest, ignoring the knowing look she sends my way. This is professional. Just doing my job. Nothing more.

The mayor's office sits at the end of the hallway, door partially open. I knock lightly on the frame, heart already accelerating like I've sprinted up stairs.

"Come in." His voice, that rough-edged baritone that does things to my insides I refuse to acknowledge.

I push the door open to find him standing at the window, hands in his pockets, silhouetted against afternoon sunlight. He turns, and for a heartbeat, his face softens with something like pleasure before his professional mask slides back into place.

"Lila. What can I do for you?"

The way he says my name—like he's tasting it—sends a warm curl through my belly. I hold up the folder like a talisman. "Budget report for the festival. And I had a question about the stage placement."

He gestures to the chair opposite his desk, moving to take his own seat. "Let's see what you've got."

I place the folder between us, flipping it open to the main projection sheet. As I explain the calculations, I'm hyperaware of him—the clean scent of his aftershave layered over that distinctive alpha musk, the way his shirtsleeves are rolled up to reveal strong forearms, the attentive tilt of his head as he listens.

"You've been thorough," he says, scanning the numbers. "More than thorough. You don't have to work quite so hard to impress me, you know."

The statement catches me off-guard. "I'm not—" I begin, then stop at the knowing arch of his eyebrow. "Okay, maybe I am. First real job, want to make a good impression."

"Consider me impressed." His mouth quirks at the corner. "Now, the stage placement?"

I pull out the site map, leaning forward to point out the current plan and my suggested alternative. He leans in too, and suddenly we're sharing the same few inches of air, his scent enveloping me, making my omega instincts purr with recognition.

"See, if we rotate it this way..." I continue, voice steady despite the heat crawling up my neck. "Better acoustics, and we don't lose any vendor space."

He nods thoughtfully, eyes still on the map. "Smart. Why wasn't this the original plan?"

"Tradition, I think. It's always been placed facing the courthouse."

"Sometimes tradition needs challenging." His gaze lifts to mine, and there it is again—that electric current jumping between us, making my skin tingle and my pulse race. His eyes drop briefly to my lips, so quickly I might have imagined it, but the intensity in his expression when he looks back up confirms I didn't.

I swallow hard. "I should get back to those vendor applications."

"Of course." He straightens, putting necessary distance between us. "Send the revised stage plan to the committee. Use my name if you meet any resistance."

I gather the materials, careful not to let our fingers brush. At the door, I pause, curiosity overriding better judgment. "Can I ask you something?"

He looks up, wary but open. "Go ahead."

"Why did you hire me? There must have been local candidates."

Something flickers in his expression—consideration, maybe even vulnerability. "Fresh perspectives keep a town from stagnating," he says finally. "You see Sanctuary with new eyes. That's valuable."

It feels like both truth and deflection. I nod, unsatisfied but unwilling to push. "Thank you for the opportunity."

"Lila." His voice stops me again, softer now. "The festival matters to this town. To me. It's... it was my wife's favorite event. I appreciate the care you're taking with it."

The confession catches me off-guard, intimate in a way our charged silences aren't. "I'll make sure it's perfect," I promise, meaning it.

He smiles then, a real smile that reaches his eyes and transforms his face. "I believe you will."

Back at my desk, I stare at my computer screen without seeing it, my body humming with awareness I can't shut down. This attraction is inappropriate, unprofessional, and completely one-sided. He's being kind to a new employee, nothing more. The electricity I feel is just omega biology responding to a compatible alpha—simple chemistry, not connection.

I force myself to open another spreadsheet, throwing myself back into work with renewed determination. Numbers don't lie. Numbers don't make my heart race or my skin flush. Numbers are safe.

But late that afternoon, I catch him watching me from across the office. Our eyes meet for a breath before he looks away too quickly, returning to his conversation with Walter as if nothing happened. But I saw it—that same hunger I'm fighting reflected in his eyes.

And for the first time, I wonder if maybe I'm not fighting alone.

That night, I dream of pine forests and smoke, of strong hands and blue eyes darkened with desire. I wake tangled in sheets, body aching with need, and curse my omega instincts for the hundredth time.

Professional. I need to be professional. He's my boss, he's older, he's still healing from loss, and I'm here to build a career, not complicate my life with inappropriate attractions.

Tomorrow, I'll bring in more spreadsheets. Tomorrow, I'll maintain proper distance. Tomorrow, I'll remember all the reasons this can never happen.

But as I fall back asleep, his scent follows me into dreams, and my resolve weakens with each breath.

4

T own Hall transforms after hours. The fluorescent buzz fades to silence. Phones stop ringing. The coffee machine gives up its death rattle. Footsteps echo through empty corridors as the last employees filter out, calling goodbyes that bounce off marble and wood. By seven o'clock, it's just me and the massive festival planning board I've spread across the conference room table, colored pins marking vendor stalls, stage positions, and security checkpoints. Founder's Festival is two weeks away, and I'm drowning in details.

I chew the end of my pen, squinting at the food truck section. Too many vendors, not enough space. Someone will have to be cut, and that someone will raise hell in this tight-knit community. Politics isn't just for governments—it's for deciding which local grandma gets prime real estate for her award-winning pie stand.

"Still at it, I see."

I startle, pen dropping from my mouth. Nate stands in the doorway, suit jacket discarded, tie loosened, sleeves rolled to expose those forearms that shouldn't be so distracting. He holds two steaming mugs, the rich scent of coffee cutting through the stale air.

"Mayor Carrington—Nate." I straighten, suddenly conscious of my rumpled blouse and the messy bun I'd twisted my hair into hours ago. "I thought everyone had left."

"Budget reports." He grimaces, stepping into the room. "Quarterly torture required by the state." He sets one mug at my elbow, the ceramic warm against my skin when our fingers brush momentarily. "Figured you could use this."

"Thanks." The coffee is exactly how I like it—one sugar, splash of cream. I don't recall ever telling him my preference. "You didn't have to stay to help with this. Festival planning is technically Samantha's committee."

He leans against the table, surveying the map. "Technically, everything in this town is my responsibility." No arrogance in the statement, just simple fact. "Besides, this festival was—" He stops, recalibrates. "It's important to me."

Was his wife's project. He doesn't need to finish the sentence for me to hear it.

"Well, I could use another set of eyes." I gesture to the food truck section. "Seven vendors, space for five. Who gets cut?"

He studies the names, sipping his coffee—black, I notice, like the circles under his eyes. "Matthews has been phoning it in the last two years. And the Hendersons are moving to Florida next month." His finger taps the pins. "Cut them, no hard feelings either way."

I make the adjustments, relieved at his decisive but thoughtful solution. We fall into an unexpected rhythm after that—me raising problems, him offering context and history I lack, us finding solutions together. The work goes faster with two, but more than that, it feels companionable in a way I hadn't anticipated.

"You've reorganized the children's area completely," he notes, examining my design.

I nod, pushing a stray hair behind my ear. "The previous layout had face painting next to the balloon animals. Disaster waiting to happen—one pop and you've got paint-streaked, screaming children."

He laughs, the sound warm and unexpected, crinkling the corners of his eyes. "Voice of experience?"

"I worked carnival booths through college." I smile at the memory. "Four summers of sticky fingers and meltdowns. You learn fast or you don't survive."

"Practical experience. That's what I liked about your application." He moves around the table, stopping to adjust a misplaced pin. "Too many interns come in with theory and no real-world knowledge."

I watch him as he leans over the map, noting how his hair falls forward when he bends, how he absently pushes it back with one hand—a small, human gesture from a man who usually seems so carefully composed. The overhead lights catch silver at his temples, more salt than pepper up close.

"What made you want to be mayor?" I ask, the late hour making me bolder than usual. "It can't have been for the glamorous budget reports."

His mouth quirks. "Certainly not for those." He straightens, considering. "I was on the council when the mining company pulled out. Town was dying. The previous mayor wanted to court big-box stores, turn us into another generic highway stop." His eyes harden with remembered determination. "I had a different vision."

"Sanctuary," I murmur.

"Yes." Something softens in his expression. "A place that preserved what mattered—community, independence, the beauty of these mountains. A place where people could feel safe." His gaze flickers to me. "Some people needed that more than others."

The statement hangs between us, weighted with meaning I'm not ready to examine. I break eye contact, moving to adjust pins that don't need adjusting.

"You've succeeded," I say finally. "This town... it feels special."

"It is." Pride warms his voice. "Though not without challenges." He checks his watch, grimacing. "Speaking of which, it's nearly nine. We should call it a night."

"Just a few more sections," I protest, not ready for this unexpected camaraderie to end. "The craft vendors still need organizing."

He studies me, head tilted. "When was the last time you ate?"

I try to remember. "Lunch? Maybe?"

"That settles it." He starts gathering his notes. "There's a pizza place three blocks down that delivers late. We'll finish the craft section while we wait."

"You don't have to—"

"I know." His eyes meet mine, direct and unguarded. "I want to."

Those three words shouldn't feel intimate, but they do. I swallow, nodding. "Pepperoni?"

"And mushroom." He's already dialing, and I wonder at this easy domesticity that's sprung up between us in the empty building.

We work through another section while waiting for the pizza, our conversation flowing more freely now, skipping between festival logistics and personal anecdotes. I learn he grew up in the next county over, that he studied urban planning before returning home, that he makes his own furniture as a hobby. Small revelations that sketch the outline of the man behind the mayoral title.

The pizza arrives, and we clear a corner of the table, paper plates and napkins creating a makeshift dining area amidst the festival plans. The casual meal loosens something between us, barriers lowering with each slice.

"So," he says, reaching for his third piece, "what really brought you to Sanctuary? And don't give me the making-a-difference line. That's true, but it's not the whole truth."

I pause, pizza halfway to my mouth. His expression is open, curious without being demanding. In the quiet of the empty building, with no one else to hear, truth feels less dangerous.

"I needed somewhere new," I say slowly. "Somewhere I could just be Lila, not someone's omega."

He nods, understanding darkening his eyes. "Bad situation?"

"Not the worst." I set down my pizza, appetite fading. "Just... suffocating. My university pack had expectations. Traditions. Roles I was supposed to fill after graduation."

"Arranged bonds?" His voice remains neutral, but a muscle tightens in his jaw.

"Strongly encouraged matches." I wrap my arms around myself, suddenly cold despite the warm room. "The alpha they picked was... traditional. Old school. Omegas in the home, barefoot and pregnant, the whole retrograde fantasy."

Nate's scent shifts subtly, a protective edge emerging that makes my inner omega sigh with recognition. "And you wanted more."

"I wanted choices." I meet his eyes, defiant even now. "My mother never had any. I watched her disappear into what everyone else needed. I refuse to do the same."

Something like admiration flashes across his face. "Good for you."

The simple validation catches me off guard. I'd expected judgment, or at least the condescending tolerance most alphas show toward "progressive" omega ideas. Instead, his approval seems genuine, unqualified.

"What about you?" I ask, deflecting attention from the warmth blooming in my chest. "After your wife... have you thought about—" I stop, horrified at my intrusive question. "I'm sorry, that's none of my business."

"It's alright." He sets down his napkin, expression thoughtful rather than offended. "Rebecca was my mate in every sense. When she died..." His hand unconsciously rubs at the pale band on his ring finger. "Some bonds don't break, even with death."

"I shouldn't have asked."

"No, it's a fair question." He meets my gaze directly. "I've dated. Nothing serious. Mostly to appease well-meaning friends who worry about me being alone." A wry smile curves his mouth. "But until recently, I haven't felt that... pull. That recognition."

Until recently. The words hang between us, charged with implication. My heart hammers against my ribs, pulse points throbbing with sudden heat. Does he mean...?

Before I can process the thought, his phone chimes with a text. He checks it, frowning.

"Sheriff needs me to sign off on festival security plan tonight." He stands, gathering his jacket. "I'm sorry to cut this short."

"No problem." I busy myself collecting pizza debris, hiding my flushed face. "Thanks for the help. And the dinner."

"We make a good team." He pauses at the door, something unspoken in his expression. "Same time tomorrow night? We could finish the rest of the sections."

I should say no. Should maintain professional distance. Should not look forward to more late nights alone with him.

"I'll be here," I say instead.

After he leaves, his scent lingers—pine, smoke, alpha, now mingled with coffee and pizza. I press my palms against the table, steadying myself as I try to make sense of what's happening between us. This connection feels dangerous, like standing at the edge of a cliff in high winds.

But as I pack up my things and switch off the lights, I can't deny the anticipation already building for tomorrow night. For more quiet conversations, more glimpses of the man behind the title, more moments when his guard drops and I see something in his eyes that mirrors the hunger growing in mine.

Professional boundaries are eroding by the hour, and the terrifying part is—I'm not sure I want to stop it.

5

The storm hits without warning. One minute we're hunched over festival security plans in the conference room, shoulders almost touching as we mark evacuation routes, and the next, the sky outside the windows turns an eerie green–black. Thunder cracks so loudly the glass rattles in its frames. I jolt upright, nearly knocking over my cold coffee. Nate glances up from the map, his expression shifting from mild curiosity to alert concern as the wind begins to howl around the old building's corners.

"That's not good." He moves to the window, scanning the darkened sky. "Summer squall. They come fast in the mountains."

I join him, keeping a careful foot of space between us—the same distance I've maintained all evening, professional and proper despite the charged atmosphere of these late-night planning sessions. Outside, trees bend sideways in the wind, leaves turned silver-side up. The first fat raindrops splatter against the glass, quickly becoming sheets of water that transform the streetlights into watery halos.

"Should we head home before it gets worse?" I ask, already knowing the answer as lightning forks across the sky, followed immediately by a boom that seems to shake the building's foundation.

Nate shakes his head. "Too late. Flash floods happen fast here. Roads will already be dangerous." His phone buzzes in his pocket. He checks it, frowning. "Sheriff's issued a shelter-in-place warning. Looks like we're stuck here for a while."

"Oh." The word comes out smaller than I intend. Trapped in the building. Alone. With him. My suppressants due hours ago.

My evening dose of suppressants is in my apartment, where I should have been an hour ago if we hadn't gotten caught up in planning. The pills I took this morning will be wearing off soon—are already weakening, if the heightened awareness of Nate's proximity is any indication.

As if on cue, the lights flicker once, twice, then plunge us into darkness.

"Perfect timing," Nate mutters. I hear him moving, the rustle of fabric as he navigates by memory. "There should be emergency lights in a second."

Dim backup lights flicker on, casting the room in shadowy blue. Nate's face appears in partial shadow, all sharp angles and hollows, more predator than mayor. My heart rate kicks up another notch.

"Are you alright?" he asks, noticing my stillness. "Not afraid of storms, are you?"

I shake my head, forcing a light tone. "No, just… I should have been home by now. I had… things to take care of."

He studies me for a moment, something shifting in his expression as understanding dawns. Alphas can scent these things—the subtle change as suppressants fade, the emerging omega pheromones no blocker can completely hide. His nostrils flare slightly, and I know he's caught it already—the first tendrils of my true scent breaking through.

"Your medication," he says quietly. Not a question.

Heat floods my face. "It's fine. I'll be fine. It's just a few hours." I move back to the table, putting furniture between us like it might help. "Let's finish this section while we wait out the storm."

He hesitates, then nods, returning to his chair. We attempt to continue working, but concentration becomes impossible as thunder cracks overhead and rain lashes the windows like it's trying to break in. The old building creaks and moans around us, pipes knocking in the walls. The backup generator hums, keeping minimal lights running but not enough to dispel the shadows that stretch across the room.

And with each passing minute, my body betrays me further.

First, it's just heightened awareness—the sound of Nate's breathing, the scratch of his pen against paper, the shift of his weight in his chair. Then my skin begins to prickle with sensitivity, my blouse suddenly abrasive against my arms. My temperature rises, a flush spreading from my chest upward. Most damning of all, my scent changes, sweetening with the first warning signs of an approaching heat.

I should have seen this coming. Stress can trigger early cycles, and between the new job, the festival pressure, and these nightly sessions with Nate, my body's been under constant strain. What should have been next week is arriving now, accelerated by circumstance and proximity to a compatible alpha.

Nate hasn't said anything, but I can tell he's noticed. His movements have become stiffer, more controlled. He keeps his distance, eyes on the papers, jaw clenched tight enough that a muscle jumps in his cheek. The conference room suddenly feels impossibly small, airless despite its size.

Another crack of thunder, so close it must have hit something nearby. The lights flicker again, and in that moment of near-darkness, Nate's scent hits me full force—pine and smoke and raw alpha need, no longer muted by my failing suppressants. A whimper escapes me before I can stop it, omega instincts responding to the call of his pheromones.

"Lila." His voice has dropped an octave, gravel over velvet. "Maybe we should… separate. Until the storm passes."

Rational. Sensible. The right call. But the thought of being alone while my body spirals toward heat sends a spike of fear through me. I've never experienced one without medication, without the controlled environment of my apartment.

"I don't—" Thunder cuts me off, and I jump, nerves frayed beyond endurance. "I can't—"

He stands abruptly, chair scraping back. "I'll go to my office. You stay here." Each word sounds forced through clenched teeth. "Lock the door."

"Nate." His name falls from my lips like a plea, though for what, I'm not entirely sure. For him to stay? To go? To make this decision for both of us?

He takes a step toward the door, then stops, hands clenching into fists at his sides. The emergency lights cast blue shadows across his face, highlighting the war being waged behind his eyes—duty versus desire, professionalism versus primal instinct.

Lightning flashes, momentarily flooding the room with brilliant white light. In that flash, I see him clearly—pupils blown wide, a thin ring of blue around bottomless black, nostrils flared as he scents my fear and arousal, chest rising and falling with too-quick breaths. He looks feral, dangerous, and so beautiful it makes my chest ache.

The following thunder shakes the building, and I tremble, sweat beading on my upper lip despite the chill from the dying air conditioning. My legs feel weak, inner thighs already slick with the first physical signs of heat. Soon I'll be past rational thought, past choice. The realization terrifies me.

"I should have been more careful," I whisper, arms wrapping around myself. "I'm sorry."

His expression softens into something pained. "Don't apologize for biology, Lila."

"I'm your intern. This is inappropriate. Unprofessional." I'm babbling now, panic rising as another wave of heat courses through me. "We can't—"

"I know." Two syllables, heavy with regret. "Which is why I need to leave. Now."

He turns toward the door again, hand reaching for the knob, and something in me breaks—omega instinct overwhelming rationality, fear of being alone in this state stronger than professional boundaries.

"Please," I gasp, the word torn from somewhere primal and desperate. "Don't leave me like this."

Nate freezes, his back to me, shoulders rigid with restraint. The air between us thickens with tension, with possibilities, with unspoken need. When he speaks, his voice is barely audible over the storm.

"If I stay, Lila... if I stay, I don't trust myself to keep my distance."

The confession hangs in the air, honest and raw. My body responds instantly, another wave of heat spreading from my core outward, omega pheromones spiking in unconscious invitation. I grip the edge of the table to stay upright, legs trembling.

"I've never—" I swallow, throat dry. "I've always been on suppressants. I don't know what's happening."

He turns slowly, and the look in his eyes steals what little breath I have left. It's hunger, yes, but also concern, protectiveness—alpha instincts to care for an omega in distress warring with his obvious desire.

"Early heat," he says, voice clinical though his scent betrays his arousal. "The storm, stress, compatible alpha proximity—all triggers."

Compatible. The word echoes through me, confirmation of what I've suspected since our first meeting—that the electricity between us isn't just attraction but something more fundamental, more dangerous. Biological recognition.

"What do we do?" I ask, hating the tremor in my voice.

Lightning flashes again, thunder following instantaneously. The lights flicker more severely this time, dipping us into near-darkness for several seconds. When they return, Nate has moved closer—not touching me, but close enough that his scent envelops me completely, making my knees weaken further.

"I can help ease the symptoms without..." He doesn't finish the sentence, doesn't need to. "Or I can lock myself in my office until morning. Your choice, Lila. Entirely your choice."

The professional boundaries I've clung to for weeks are crumbling like sandcastles in the tide of my approaching heat. I know what the right decision is—the one that protects my career, his position, the careful distance we've maintained despite the pull between us.

But as another cramp seizes my abdomen and lightning cracks overhead, mirroring the electricity arcing between us, right and wrong blur into meaningless abstractions. All that remains is need—and the only alpha I've ever truly wanted standing before me, offering comfort I've never allowed myself to imagine.

"Stay," I whisper, the single word carrying the weight of surrender. "Please stay."

6

The storm outside has nothing on the one raging inside me. Heat crashes through my system in merciless waves, each one stronger than the last. My skin burns everywhere, sensitive to the point of pain. Slick dampens my thighs, and my scent has transformed completely—honey and cinnamon and raw omega need filling the room despite the blockers I applied this morning. I can't think straight, can barely stand as another cramp seizes my abdomen, dragging a whimper from my throat.

Nate remains a few feet away, his restraint visible in the rigid set of his shoulders, the white-knuckled fists at his sides. His eyes have gone dark, pupils swallowing the blue, but he hasn't moved since I asked him to stay. The last threads of his control are visible in the tremor of his hands, the muscle jumping in his jaw.

"Tell me what you need," he says, voice barely human—all alpha rumble that vibrates through my bones.

What I need. What I need is him, his hands, his mouth, his body against mine. What I need is relief from this consuming fire. What I need is something I've never allowed myself to have—surrender to instinct without shame.

"I'm scared," I admit, the confession torn from somewhere raw and honest. "I've never felt it this strongly. I can't—I don't know how to—" Another wave hits, stronger than before, forcing me to grip the table edge to stay upright. "Please, Nate. Help me."

Something breaks in his expression at my plea—the last barrier of professional restraint crumbling under the weight of alpha instinct. He moves toward me with predatory grace, and my omega responds instantly, body softening in anticipation even as my mind races with last-minute doubts.

"This isn't just the heat talking?" he asks, stopping just short of touching me, his scent wrapping around me like a physical caress. "Because once I touch you, Lila, I don't think I can stop."

The raw honesty in his voice cuts through the haze of my heat. Even now, trembling with need, he's giving me a choice. Respect beneath desire. I've never had that before—never had an alpha who saw me as more than omega biology.

I reach for him, fingers curling into his shirt front.

"I've wanted you since the first day," I confess. "The heat just burned away my restraint."

It's all the permission he needs. His mouth claims mine with bruising intensity, swallowing my gasp of relief. The first touch of his lips sends electricity down my spine, my body arching into his as his arms finally, finally wrap around me. He tastes of coffee and thunder, of alpha need barely leashed.

His hands are everywhere, urgent yet careful—sliding up my sides, tangling in my hair, cupping my face as he deepens the kiss. I respond with equal fervor, weeks of denied attraction exploding into desperate need. My fingers fumble with his shirt buttons, needing skin contact like I need air.

"Too many clothes," I mutter against his mouth.

He makes a sound of agreement, breaking the kiss to work at my blouse. His fingers tremble slightly as he undoes each button, revealing inches of flushed skin to his hungry gaze. When he pushes the fabric from my shoulders, the cool air makes me shiver, nipples tightening against the lace of my bra. His eyes darken further as he takes me in.

"Beautiful," he breathes, hands hovering just above my skin, as though afraid I'll break. "You're so beautiful it hurts to look at you."

Thunder crashes outside, and the emergency lights flicker. In that moment of semi-darkness, something primal takes over—my omega reaching for his alpha, biology overriding hesitation. I press against him, skin to skin where his shirt hangs open, and the contact draws a growl from deep in his chest.

"My office," he manages, voice strained. "More private."

He leads me down the darkened hallway, my hand clasped in his, heat pulsing between my thighs with each step. His office door clicks shut behind us, and he locks it with shaking fingers before turning back to me.

I've imagined this moment in guilty dreams—Nate's hands on my body, his mouth on my skin. The reality is both more intense and more tender than fantasy. He undresses me with reverent efficiency, each newly revealed inch of skin worshipped with calloused fingertips and hot, open-mouthed kisses. By the time I stand naked before him, I'm trembling uncontrollably, slick coating my thighs, need a physical ache deep in my core.

"Nate, please." I'm beyond pride, beyond restraint. "I need you now."

Something flashes in his eyes—possessiveness, hunger, something deeper I can't name. He shrugs out of his shirt, revealing a broad chest dusted with dark hair, scattered scars telling stories of a life lived fully. I reach out to trace one that runs along his ribs, fascinated despite my urgency.

"Later," he promises, catching my hand and bringing it to his lips. "I'll let you explore every inch later. But right now—"

He doesn't finish the sentence, doesn't need to. In one fluid movement, he lifts me onto his desk, scattering papers and pens that clatter to the floor unheeded. His hands push my thighs apart, making space for his body between them. I should feel exposed, vulnerable, but all I feel is desperate anticipation as he works at his belt, freeing himself from confining fabric.

The first press of his cock against my entrance draws a broken sound from my throat—relief and need and plea all at once. He pauses, eyes finding mine in the dim blue light.

"Are you sure?" he asks, one last check despite the evidence of my body's readiness.

"Yes." I wrap my legs around his hips, drawing him closer. "God, yes."

He enters me in one long, deliberate thrust that steals the breath from my lungs. The stretch and fullness is overwhelming, perfect, exactly what my heat-drunk body craves. My back arches off the desk, a high keening sound escaping me as he fills me completely.

"Fuck, Lila." His voice breaks on my name, hands gripping my hips hard enough to bruise. "You feel—you're perfect."

I can't respond, can barely think as he begins to move. Each thrust sends sparks of pleasure up my spine, my body responding to his as though made for this purpose. His rhythm is steady but relentless, driving me higher with each stroke. My nails dig into his shoulders, leaving crescent marks that my omega instincts thrill to see on his skin.

The storm outside reaches its crescendo as we find our rhythm—lightning flashing through the half-closed blinds, thunder shaking the building's foundations. Nate bends to capture my mouth again, swallowing my moans as his pace increases. One hand slides between us, thumb finding my clit with unerring accuracy, circling in time with his thrusts.

"That's it," he murmurs against my lips. "Let go for me, omega."

The command in his voice, the use of my designation rather than my name—it triggers something primal in me. Heat coils tighter in my core, pressure building to impossible levels. I feel the beginnings of his knot stretching me further with each thrust, the distinctive swell that marks an alpha in rut.

"I'm going to—" I can't even finish the sentence as pleasure crashes over me, whiting out thought, arching my body against his. I come with a cry that might be his name, inner muscles clamping down on him as wave after wave of release pulses through me.

Nate follows moments later, his rhythm faltering as his knot locks into place. He buries his face against my neck, teeth grazing the sensitive skin where my scent is strongest. Not biting—not claiming—but close enough that my omega instincts sing with near-completion. He groans my name as he comes, the sound reverent and broken, his body shuddering against mine.

For long moments afterward, the only sounds are our ragged breathing and the rain against the windows. The storm outside has begun to ease, thunder now distant rumblings rather than world-shaking crashes. Nate's weight presses me into the desk, his knot binding us together in the most intimate way possible. I should feel trapped, but instead, I feel anchored—safe in the aftermath of my heat's most intense wave.

His hand comes up to stroke my hair, gentle in contrast to the desperation of moments before. "Are you alright?" he whispers against my temple.

I nod, not trusting my voice yet. Alright doesn't begin to cover the complexity of what I'm feeling—satiated yet hungry for more, physically fulfilled yet emotionally raw, terrified of what we've done yet unable to regret it.

Carefully, mindful of our joined bodies, Nate shifts us into his office chair, cradling me in his lap as we wait for his knot to recede. The position is intimate, tender, his arms wrapped protectively around me as aftershocks of pleasure ripple through my body.

"I didn't plan this," he says finally, voice quiet in the dim office. "I need you to know that."

I lift my head from his shoulder to meet his gaze. His eyes have returned to their normal blue, concern replacing the alpha haze of earlier.

"I know," I assure him. "Neither did I."

His thumb traces my lower lip, tender now where he was desperate before. "This changes things."

"Yes." There's no denying it, no going back to professional distance after what we've shared.

"I should regret it," he continues, forehead pressing against mine. "For your sake, for the town's, I should regret it."

"But you don't?" I ask, suddenly unsure despite the evidence of our still-joined bodies.

His lips brush mine, a whisper of a kiss compared to our earlier frenzy. "Not for a second," he admits. "And that terrifies me more than you know."

Lightning flashes once more, illuminating his face—the vulnerability there, the wonder, the fear that mirrors my own. In this moment, stripped of titles and clothing alike, we're just a man and woman caught in a storm of their own making.

And as his knot finally eases and our bodies separate, I know with bone-deep certainty that though the rain may stop and morning will come, nothing between us will ever be the same again.

7

The office floor isn't comfortable, but neither of us makes any move to leave. Nate had the presence of mind to pull the ancient wool rug from under his desk and spread it beneath us after the second time, creating a makeshift nest against the hardwood. Now we lie tangled together, my head on his chest, his fingers tracing idle patterns on my bare back. The storm has gentled to steady rain against the windows, a rhythmic backdrop to our slowing heartbeats. My heat has ebbed to a manageable warmth, sated temporarily by his touch.

In the blue glow of the emergency lights, Nate's body is a landscape of shadows and planes. I explore him with curious fingers, learning him by touch now that urgency has given way to tenderness. His chest rises and falls beneath my palm, steady and strong. Coarse hair tickles my skin as I trace the defined muscles of his torso—a body kept fit by more than just appearance's sake, functional strength rather than vanity.

I shift to see his face better, propping myself on an elbow. "You're full of surprises, Mayor Carrington."

Something vulnerable flickers in his eyes. "I'm still discovering them myself."

My fingers continue their exploration, discovering a map of his life written in scars and muscle memory. Each mark has a story, each callus a purpose. He's lived in this body fully, using it to build and protect and rescue. Nothing like the soft, manicured alphas from my university pack, whose only physical exertions came from the gym and bedroom conquests.

When my hand drifts lower, tracing the cut of muscle at his hip, his breath catches. His own hand captures mine, bringing it to his lips. "Not yet," he murmurs against my fingertips. "Let me look at you first."

He shifts our positions with gentle hands, laying me back against the makeshift nest, hovering above me with eyes that seem to memorize every detail. Where my touch was curious, his is reverent—fingertips skimming my collarbones, palm cupping my breast with tender appreciation, thumb brushing across ribs as though counting each one to ensure none are broken.

"You're so young," he whispers, more to himself than to me. "So full of possibility."

I frown at the edge in his voice. "I'm twenty-two, not seventeen. Old enough to know what I want."

"It's not that." He shakes his head, hand still moving in gentle exploration. "It's that you have so many paths still open to you. A whole future waiting. And I'm..."

"What?" I reach up to touch his face, feeling the stubble that's emerged over our long night. "Established? Respected? Secure in who you are?"

A shadow crosses his expression. "Damaged. Set in my ways. Still half in love with a ghost."

The confession hangs between us, honest and raw. His hand stills on my skin, as though expecting rejection now that he's revealed this truth.

Instead, I pull him down to me, our bodies aligning in a way that already feels familiar. "We're all damaged," I whisper against his lips. "I'm not asking for perfection. Just honesty."

Something breaks in his expression—relief, perhaps, or surrender. He kisses me with aching tenderness, so different from our earlier desperation. This kiss speaks of care rather than possession, appreciation rather than need. His weight settles against me, comforting rather than restricting, and I open for him like a flower turning toward sunlight.

He takes his time as he enters me, the anticipation measured in heartbeats and the tiny, involuntary shudders that chase up my spine. We are no longer lost to instinct—each movement is an exercise in restraint and reverence, a deliberate savoring of the moment. His hand cradles my jaw, thumb stroking the fine line of my cheekbone as he guides himself into me with infinite patience. The sensation is exquisite—nothing muffled or blunted by heat-madness, every nerve alive to the lithe press of his body against mine.

I gasp, sharp and soft, as the first inch slides in. The fit is intimate, a sensation I had never thought could be so detailed, so nuanced. I feel the tension in his thighs and the way his arms tremble not from exertion but from an effort to prolong this, to keep from crushing me beneath the weight of his longing. His eyes are fixed on me, not on my body but on my face, as if searching for something deeper than permission—affirmation, acceptance, maybe even forgiveness. I give it in the way I tilt my hips to welcome him, in the knotted fingers grasping his shoulders, in the sigh that escapes me as he sheathes himself fully.

He holds himself there, motionless for a moment, the intimacy of it turning the air electric. My hands roam over the solid curve of his back, the ridges of muscle that flex beneath my touch. I want to memorize him the way he's memorizing me, to learn the language of his body in this new, gentle dialect. The rain outside is a metronome to our joined breaths, the distant thunder a reminder that the world is still out there, but somewhere far away.

Nate brushes a strand of hair from my face, his fingers feather-light.

"Does it hurt?" he asks, his voice a low caress, the words edged with genuine concern.

"Only in the best way," I whisper, finding his hand with mine and lacing our fingers together. I guide his palm to my sternum, where my heart drums with frantic certainty.

He begins to move, slow and shallow at first, and the sensation is so different—so colored by intention and connection—that I nearly sob with the intensity of it. Gone is the frantic clashing of heat and rut; what fills the space between us now is something reverent, almost holy. He kisses me, soft and unhurried, and it feels as though he's tasting every regret, every fear, every hope I have ever harbored. My legs wrap around him, heels pressing into the small of his back, drawing him closer still.

His rhythm is a slow build, each thrust coaxing a new wave of sensation that crests and breaks with devastating tenderness. His lips trace a line from my mouth to my jaw, down the column of my throat to the hollow at its base, leaving heat in their wake. I arch into him, greedy for the friction, the pressure, the promise of release held at bay for as long as we can bear it. His free hand smoothes the inside of my thigh, thumb circling idly atop my trembling skin.

"Nate," I gasp, the name a prayer and a promise.

He groans in response, the sound vibrating through both of us. He buries his face in the crook of my neck, teeth grazing but not breaking skin, his scent so thick around me I could drown in it. The slow grind of his hips is maddening, pleasure building in gradual, dizzy increments. I cling to his broad shoulders, feeling the echo of every movement in the deepest part of me.

He lifts his head just enough to look at me, pupils blown wide, blue irises ringed with gold in the low light.

"You're beautiful," he murmurs, eyes never leaving mine as he begins to move. "So beautiful it hurts."

No one has ever looked at me this way before—like I'm something precious, something to be cherished rather than just desired. His rhythm remains unhurried, deep strokes that reach places inside me I didn't know existed. My hands find purchase on his shoulders, not clinging in desperation as before, but holding in wonder.

"I'm sorry," he whispers against my temple, the words so quiet I almost miss them beneath the sound of rain.

"For what?" I gasp as he hits a particularly sensitive spot, pleasure spiraling outward from my center.

"For wanting this." His voice breaks slightly. "For not being stronger. For taking what I have no right to claim."

I cradle his face between my palms, forcing him to meet my gaze even as our bodies continue their gentle dance.

"I wanted this too," I remind him. "I still want it. I want you."

Something shifts in his expression—hope warring with doubt, desire with self-recrimination. He increases his pace slightly, one hand sliding between us to where we're joined, thumb circling the bundle of nerves that makes me arch beneath him.

"Then have me," he says, voice rough with emotion. "All of me, Lila. Even the broken parts."

It's this—this offer of vulnerability rather than just his body—that pushes me over the edge. My release washes through me in gentle waves, not the violent storm of before but something deeper, more profound. I cling to him as it takes me, his name a prayer on my lips.

He follows moments later, face buried against my neck, his body shuddering above mine. No knot this time—his rut as temporarily sated as my heat—just the warm pulse of his release inside me, binding us together in the most ancient way.

Afterward, he gathers me close, pulling his discarded shirt over me against the chill of the air-conditioning that has begun to work again as power flickers back to life. The office lights remain off, leaving us in comfortable semi-darkness broken only by the occasional flash of distant lightning.

"I've never done this before," I confess into the quiet.

His hand stills in my hair. "Been with an alpha?"

"Been with anyone like this." I trace patterns on his chest, suddenly shy despite our intimacy. "I've dated, but never... felt this."

"This?" he prompts, voice carefully neutral.

I struggle to find words for the bone-deep recognition, the sense of rightness that persists even beyond the heat-haze. "Like I've found something I didn't know I was missing."

His arms tighten around me, and I feel him press a kiss to the top of my head. "I know exactly what you mean."

We talk then, in the hushed tones of new lovers, about everything and nothing. He tells me about growing up in these mountains, about meeting Rebecca in college, about the painful years after her death when the town became his only purpose. I tell him about my domineering pack, my mother's quiet submission that I vowed never to repeat, my dreams of making something meaningful of my life.

Simple confidences exchanged in the dark, building bridges between our separate worlds. His fingers never stop their gentle exploration—tracing my spine, the curve of my hip, the line of my jaw—as though he's committing me to memory through touch.

"What happens tomorrow?" I ask finally, the question that's been hovering at the edges of my consciousness.

His chest rises and falls with a deep breath.

"I don't know," he admits. "Nothing in the handbook covers this scenario."

I smile against his skin. "Is there an actual handbook? For mayors?"

"Three of them. None helpful." His attempt at humor doesn't quite mask the concern in his voice. "This will complicate things."

"I know." I prop myself up again to see his face, needing to gauge his reaction. "Do you regret it?"

His eyes meet mine, steady and clear in the dim light.

"I should," he says honestly. "For your sake, for the town's, I should regret every minute." His hand cups my cheek, thumb brushing my lower lip. "But I don't. And that terrifies me more than anything has in years."

The simple truth of his words wraps around my heart like a fist. I turn my face to press a kiss into his palm, unable to articulate the tangle of emotions his confession evokes.

Outside, the storm continues to recede, thunder now just distant rumblings. Inside, wrapped in Nate's arms on the uncomfortable floor of his office, I feel safer than I ever have before. My eyelids grow heavy, the combination of emotional and physical exertion finally catching up to me.

"Sleep," he murmurs, noticing my struggle to stay awake. "I'll keep watch."

"The storm..." I protest weakly.

"Is passing." He pulls me closer, arranging us more comfortably on our makeshift bed. "Rest while your heat lets you. I'll be here."

As I drift toward sleep, his heartbeat steady beneath my ear, the outside world with all its complications seems very far away. Tomorrow will bring consequences, judgments, difficult conversations. But tonight, in the quiet aftermath of the storm, we've carved out a sanctuary within Sanctuary—a private world where nothing exists beyond the touch of skin on skin and the whispered truths we've shared.

I know it can't last. But as sleep claims me, wrapped in Nate's scent and warmth, I let myself believe—just for these precious hours—that what

we've found might be worth whatever price awaits
us in the morning light.

8

Sunlight stabs through the office blinds, slicing across my face like an accusation. I jerk awake, disoriented by the hard floor beneath me, the wool rug scratching my bare skin. For a moment, I can't place where I am—then it all rushes back in vivid, sense-memory detail. The storm. My heat. Nate's hands, his mouth, his body moving with mine. I bolt upright, sheet clutched to my chest, heart hammering with fight-or-flight adrenaline. But the office is empty. Nate is gone.

His dress shirt covers me like a makeshift nightgown, the fabric still carrying his scent—pine, smoke, alpha, sex. But the man himself has vanished. No note. No explanation. Just the echo of whispered intimacies that now feel like lies in the harsh morning light.

"Nate?" My voice sounds small in the empty office, already knowing there won't be an answer.

I stand on shaky legs, wrapping the shirt tighter around me, suddenly aware of every ache and tender spot—physical reminders of what we shared. The clock on the wall reads 7:12 AM. Early enough that the building should still be empty, late enough that Nate has had plenty of time to reconsider everything that happened between us.

The evidence of his departure surrounds me—desk straightened, papers stacked neatly in the corner, festival plans rolled and secured with a rubber band. Even the carpet has been vacuumed, erasing all signs of our lovemaking except those marked on my body. It's as though he's tried to erase last night entirely, sanitizing the office of our indiscretion.

Only my clothes, folded in a neat pile on his chair, betray that anything unusual happened here.

I dress, each button and zip a reclamation of the professional identity that dissolved in last night's storm. My blouse smells faintly of Nate despite his efforts, his scent embedded in the fabric after being pressed against his bare skin. My hair is beyond saving—I twist it into a messy bun, not caring that it screams "morning after" to anyone with eyes.

His shirt lies on the floor where I dropped it, navy blue against the beige carpet. I should leave it there for him to find, a reminder he can't erase so easily. Instead, I fold it carefully, placing it on his desk chair. Let him deal with returning it or disposing of it. I won't play the omega stereotype, clinging to an alpha's possessions for comfort.

The building remains silent as I gather my things and slip out of his office. No security guards, no early-arriving clerks. Small mercies. The hallway stretches before me, a gauntlet I must walk with my dignity wrapped around me like armor.

By the time I push through the main doors into the morning sunshine, I've constructed a mask of composure—spine straight, chin level, expression carefully neutral. The air outside is fresh and clean after the storm, puddles on the sidewalk reflecting a cloudless sky. Nature showing no evidence of last night's violence, just as Town Hall shows no evidence of what happened within its walls.

Three blocks. That's all that stands between me and the privacy of my apartment, where I can finally process the tangle of emotions threatening to choke me. Three blocks of public exposure in a town where everyone knows everyone's business.

I make it halfway down the first block before I notice the stares. A pair of women outside the bakery, heads bent together, eyes following me as I pass. The postman, pausing in his rounds to watch me with undisguised curiosity. The hardware store owner, sweeping his front step, who actually stops mid-motion to track my progress down the sidewalk.

They know. Somehow, they already know.

I keep walking, each step a conscious effort not to break into a run. My scent, despite a hasty application of blockers found in my purse, must still carry traces of Nate and sex and heat. To the heightened senses of alphas and even some betas, I might as well be wearing a neon sign.

"—mayor's office all night—"

"—during the storm—"

"—barely older than his daughter would be—"

The fragments of whispered gossip reach me as I pass the diner, where the morning crowd has spilled onto the sidewalk tables. I don't slow, don't acknowledge the sudden hush that falls as I walk by. But inside, something cracks—the first hairline fracture in the shell of composure I've built around myself.

Shame burns hot under my skin, followed immediately by a wave of anger that surprises me with its intensity. What right do they have to judge? What do they know of what passed between Nate and me? Of the tenderness in his touch, the vulnerability in his eyes as he held me after?

But I know how it looks—young omega intern, older alpha boss, a convenient storm trapping them together. The power imbalance. The cliché. The assumption that I used my biology to advance my career, or that he took advantage of his position to satisfy his urges.

Neither truth fits what happened between us.

By the time I reach my apartment building, my hands are shaking with suppressed emotion. I fumble with the key, cursing under my breath as it sticks in the lock. Once inside, I lean against the door, eyes closed, breathing through the tightness in my chest.

The shower I take is scalding hot, as if I could wash away not just Nate's scent but the judgment in those stares, the speculation in those whispers. But as I stand under the spray, something shifts inside me—the hurt of waking alone transforming into clarity.

Last night wasn't just biology. It wasn't just my heat or his rut or convenient proximity during a storm. What I felt in his arms—what I still feel despite his absence this morning—goes beyond physical attraction or omega instinct.

I've never felt so seen by anyone, so understood on a level that transcends designation. The way he looked at me in those quiet moments after, like I was precious and terrifying in equal measure. The way he touched me, not just with desire but with reverence. The way he listened to my dreams as if they mattered as much as his own.

That wasn't just sex. That was connection. That was recognition.

And he's running from it.

The realization brings a bitter laugh to my lips as I shut off the water. Of course he's running. A widower who's poured his entire life into this town suddenly faced with unexpected feelings for a woman fifteen years his junior? His intern, no less? The complications alone would send anyone running for the hills.

But I'm tired of running. Tired of hiding what I want behind propriety and expectations. I left my old pack to escape that life—to find somewhere I could be myself without apology.

As I towel off and dress in clean clothes, a new resolve settles in my bones. I won't play the heartbroken omega, pining after an alpha who couldn't face morning-after consequences. But I won't pretend last night meant nothing either.

If Nate wants to pretend nothing happened, that's his choice. But he'll have to do it to my face. He'll have to look me in the eyes and tell me he regrets everything. That the words we whispered, the promises implied in each touch, were meaningless.

I don't think he can. I saw too much truth in his eyes last night, felt too much honesty in his hands.

Let the town gossip. Let them speculate and judge. They don't know what passed between us in those quiet hours after the storm. They don't know the man behind the mayor's title any more than they know the woman behind my omega designation.

But I do. I know him now—have traced his scars with my fingers, tasted the salt of his skin, felt him tremble with vulnerability in my arms. And he knows me—not just my body, but my fears, my dreams, the determination that brought me to Sanctuary.

That knowledge can't be erased by an empty office or neatly stacked papers. It lives in us now, real and undeniable.

As the morning advances and my heat simmers down to manageable levels, I make coffee and force myself to eat, preparing for whatever comes next. The town's judgment. Nate's regret. Professional fallout.

Let it come. I've survived worse than public disapproval. I've survived being told my dreams were inappropriate for an omega, that my desires were secondary to my biology, that my worth was measured by which alpha claimed me.

Sanctuary was supposed to be different. Nate was supposed to be different.

9

Two days of whispers, stares, and pointed silence have worn my determination to paper-thin fragments. I pace my apartment like a caged animal, the walls closing in with each turn. Enough. If Nate won't face me, I'll damn well make him. I grab my keys, slam the door behind me, and step into the darkness with purpose burning through my veins.

The drive to Nate's house takes me beyond town limits, up winding mountain roads where streetlights give way to star-spattered darkness. I've never been here before, but everyone knows where the mayor lives—the old Carrington farmhouse on the eastern ridge, passed down through generations before becoming his sanctuary after Rebecca died.

Gravel crunches beneath my tires as I pull into his driveway. The house looms before me—two stories of weathered clapboard and sturdy beams, warm light spilling from downstairs windows. A porch wraps around the front, rocking chairs swaying gently in the night breeze. It looks like something from a painting—the quintessential mountain home, isolated and self-sufficient. Like its owner.

I kill the engine but sit gripping the steering wheel, second thoughts crowding in now that I'm actually here. What if he refuses to see me? What if he's not alone? What if—

No. No more what-ifs. I didn't leave my pack, my past, everything I knew just to become a cowering omega again. I deserve answers, explanations, truth. I climb out of the car, slamming the door with more force than necessary, and march up the porch steps.

Three sharp knocks. My heart hammers against my ribs as I wait, each second stretching into infinity.

The door swings open, and there he is—disheveled and beautiful in worn jeans and a faded t-shirt, feet bare against hardwood floors. His hair is mussed like he's been running his hands through it, dark shadows smudged beneath his eyes. He looks like he hasn't slept since I saw him last.

His expression shifts from surprise to wariness to something like pain. "Lila." My name comes out rough, like it hurts to say. "It's late."

"Is it?" I push past him into the house, not waiting for an invitation. "I hadn't noticed. Time gets strange when you're the center of town gossip."

He closes the door slowly, as though buying time. "I meant to call you."

"When?" I spin to face him, anger bubbling up like lava. "Before or after everyone in town had dissected our personal business? Before or after Claire Jensen looked at me like I was something she scraped off her shoe?"

He winces. "I'm sorry. I didn't think—"

"No, you didn't think!" My voice rises despite my efforts to control it. "You didn't think about what would happen when you disappeared. When you left me alone in your office like some dirty secret you needed to scrub away!"

"That's not—" He drags a hand down his face. "I was trying to protect you."

"Bullshit." The word explodes from me, sharp and unfiltered. "You were protecting yourself. Your reputation. Your precious town image."

His eyes flash, alpha frustration bleeding into his scent. "You think that's what I care about? My image?"

"I don't know what you care about!" I throw my hands up. "You showed me one thing in that office—with your hands, your mouth, your words—and then something entirely different when you vanished before I woke up!"

"I care about YOU!" He steps closer, voice dropping to that alpha timber that resonates in my bones. "I left because if I'd stayed, if I'd watched you wake up in my arms, I wouldn't have been able to walk away at all. And you deserve better than this—than me."

"Don't you dare tell me what I deserve." I jab a finger at his chest. "I'm so sick of alphas deciding what's best for me without bothering to ask what I want!"

"What do you want, then?" He catches my wrist, not restraining, just connecting. His touch sends electricity up my arm. "Tell me, Lila. Because all I see is ways I complicate your life. I'm your boss. I'm fifteen years older. I'm the mayor of a town that's currently treating you like a pariah because of me!"

"I want you to stop hiding!" The words tear from somewhere raw and honest inside me. "I want you to admit what happened between us wasn't just biology or convenience or a mistake!"

His jaw clenches, muscles working beneath stubbled skin. "It wasn't a mistake," he says, voice low and strained. "That's the problem."

Something hot and desperate rises in me, frustration and need tangling until I can't separate them. I shove at his chest, hard enough that he steps back. "Then why are you acting like it was? Why did you leave? Why have you avoided me for two days while I faced the judgment of your precious town alone?"

He doesn't answer, just stares at me with too many emotions warring in his eyes. The silence stretches between us, taut and vibrating like a plucked string.

I shove him again, palm flat against his solid chest. "Say something!"

His control snaps like a dam breaking. In one fluid motion, he catches my wrists, spins me around, and presses me against the wall. His mouth crashes into mine, desperate and consuming. I respond instantly, anger transmuting to desire as our lips and teeth and tongues clash in a battle neither of us wants to win.

His hands release my wrists to tangle in my hair, cradling my head as the kiss softens from fury to hunger. My own hands fist in his shirt, pulling him closer until there's not a molecule of air between us. He tastes like need so potent it makes me dizzy.

"I can't stop thinking about you," he murmurs against my lips, the confession torn from him like it hurts. "I can't sleep. Can't focus. Can't breathe without remembering your scent."

I nip at his lower lip, drawing a growl from deep in his chest. "Then stop fighting it."

Something primal flares in his eyes. He lifts me as though I weigh nothing, my legs automatically wrapping around his waist as he carries me through the house. The kitchen counter meets my back, cool granite against heated skin as he sets me down, hands already working at my clothes.

There's no slow exploration this time, no gentle discovery. We tear at each other like starving creatures, buttons flying, fabric ripping. His mouth blazes a trail down my neck, teeth grazing the sensitive juncture of neck and shoulder—so close to where a mating bite would go that my omega instincts whimper in recognition.

"Need you," he growls, hands gripping my hips as he positions himself. "Now."

"Yes," I gasp, beyond pride, beyond restraint. "Please, Nate."

His hands span my hips, grip unyielding, every inch of his body crowding out hesitation and doubt. The world shrinks to the press of his chest to mine, to the sharp sting where his stubble grazes my jaw, to the ache between my legs as he positions himself, eyes locked on me with a hunger so fierce it's almost painful.

He doesn't ask, doesn't coax—he claims. One deep, irrevocable thrust splits me open, jaw wrenching a cry from my throat that drowns even the storm pounding behind my ribs. My head knocks back, spine arcing, lungs struggling to keep pace with the sudden incineration of need. It's not careful, not orchestrated, not the tender romance I sometimes pictured in lonely midnight hours.

It's furious and honest and completely, utterly necessary.

He buries his face in my shoulder, the heat of his breath a feral counterpoint to the relentless rhythm of his hips. Each slam of his body into mine rattles the glassware off the countertop, the force of it echoing in the bones of the house. Somewhere in the too-bright kitchen, a clock ticks absurdly, counting off seconds that feel like years. His hands slip beneath me, lifting my ass off the polished granite, angling me so there's no resistance, no room to hide, no way to pretend I'm not just as desperate as he is.

"Nate," I gasp, the name expelled on a ragged shudder. His teeth scrape the curve of my throat, and my omega instincts rear up, shuddering in anticipation for a bite that never quite lands. He's holding back—still fighting the part of himself that wants to mark me, to make this more permanent than either of us is prepared to admit.

His restraint breaks me. I reach for his face, force his gaze to mine, let him see the tears pooling at the corners of my eyes—not from pain, but from relief. From the overwhelming rightness of being shattered by this particular man.

"Let go," I whisper, voice so thin it's almost not there. "Please, Nate—don't hold back."

His eyes blaze, pupils blown wide, the blue nearly swallowed by black. He surrenders to the plea without another word. The tempo ratchets up, each thrust slamming my body into the edge of the counter. The cold granite is nothing compared to the fire between us, the raw friction of skin and heat and sweat. I clutch at his shoulders, nails digging half-moons into flesh as I climb, and climb, and finally break apart around him. The orgasm hits like a landslide—unstoppable, all-consuming, every nerve ending singing with release.

He doesn't stop—not even when I spasm and twist in his grip, not even when my voice gives out. He chases his own undoing, a snarl of need distorting his beautiful mouth as he slams into me, once, twice, and then freezes. He buries himself to the hilt, trembling, the force of his climax wringing a raw, unguarded sound from his chest. I feel the heat of him, the fullness, the irreducible truth of what we are in this moment. A mess of need and emotion, tangled together in defiance of everything the world expects.

The house is silent except for the ragged sounds of our breathing, the tick of the kitchen clock, and the soft patter of rain against the window. We don't move. I'm still impaled on him, body shaking in the aftermath, arms wrapped around his neck like if I let go, I'll fall into the void.

He leans his forehead against mine, sweat slicking our skin, his hands gentling their grip even as he keeps me anchored to him. I expect shame, or regret, or at least the old hesitation to creep back in. But when his eyes meet mine, all I see is awe, and longing, and terror.

For long moments afterward, we stay joined, breath mingling, hearts hammering against each other through slick skin. His forehead rests against mine, eyes closed as though he can't bear to look at me yet.

When he finally pulls back, lifting me gently from the counter and setting me on my feet, his expression has shifted from desire to something raw and vulnerable. He doesn't let me go, keeping me within the circle of his arms as he finds words.

"I'm terrified," he admits, voice barely above a whisper. "Of this. Of us. Of what I feel when I'm with you."

I reach up to touch his face, fingertips tracing the stubble along his jaw. "Tell me why."

He closes his eyes briefly, leaning into my touch. "I wasn't supposed to feel this way again. After Rebecca... I put everything into this town. It was safer that way. Loving a person—it leaves you exposed. Vulnerable." His voice catches. "When she died, it nearly destroyed me. I can't go through that again."

"I'm not asking you to," I whisper, though part of me aches at the thought that he's holding back.

"But you deserve someone whole." His hand cups my cheek, thumb brushing across my lower lip.

"Not someone half-living in the past, afraid of the future."

"I deserve someone honest." I hold his gaze, refusing to let him look away. "Someone who sees me—really sees me—not just as an omega or an intern or a body to warm their bed."

"I see you, Lila." The simple truth in his voice makes my chest tight. "That's what scares me most. I thought those parts of me were dead, but you've woken them up. And now I don't know how to go back to living without them. Without you."

I stretch up on tiptoes, pressing my lips to his—a gentle kiss, not of passion but promise. "Then don't try."

He holds me tighter, as though afraid I might disappear. In the quiet of his kitchen, with moonlight spilling through windows and our clothes scattered across the floor, we stand exposed in more ways than one—raw, vulnerable, finally honest about what's growing between us.

10

Morning light filters through unfamiliar curtains, painting gold streaks across a bedroom I'm still learning. Nate sleeps beside me, one arm thrown protectively over my waist, his face softened in sleep to reveal the man beneath the mayor's burden. I trace the silver at his temples with gentle fingers, memorizing the terrain of his face. Yesterday, I came here angry and hurt; today, I wake with purpose crystallizing in my bones. No more hiding. No more shame. What we've found is worth defending, even against an entire town's judgment.

His eyes flutter open, finding mine instantly. For a moment, fear flickers across his face—as though he expects me to have vanished, or to regret everything in the harsh light of day. Then I smile, and the tension melts from his shoulders.

"You're still here," he murmurs, voice rough with sleep.

"Did you think I wouldn't be?"

His hand finds mine, thumb tracing circles against my palm. "I wouldn't have blamed you. There's still time to walk away from this. From me."

I prop myself up on one elbow, making sure he sees the certainty in my eyes. "I'm not walking away, Nate. Not unless you ask me to."

He pulls me closer, burying his face against my neck, inhaling deeply as though trying to embed my scent in his memory. "I don't want you to go. But I need you to understand what you're in for. This town—"

"Will talk. Will judge. Will make assumptions." I pull back to meet his gaze. "They're already doing it. Hiding just gives them more ammunition, makes it seem like we have something to be ashamed of."

His brow furrows. "It's not about shame. It's about protecting you."

"I don't need protection," I say firmly. "I need a partner. Someone who stands beside me, not in front of me."

He studies me for a long moment, something like admiration dawning in his eyes. "You're extraordinary, you know that? Most people would be looking for a way out of this mess."

"This isn't a mess." I cup his face between my palms. "This is a beginning. Isn't that what

Sanctuary is all about? Second chances? New beginnings?"

A smile tugs at the corner of his mouth. "Using my own town's ethos against me? That's fighting dirty."

"I'll use whatever works." I lean in to press a quick kiss to his lips. "You built this place so people could start over, find safety, build the lives they want. Don't we deserve that too?"

His arms tighten around me, and I can feel the moment something shifts in him—resistance giving way to resolve. "You're right. Hiding goes against everything I've tried to create here." He sighs, forehead resting against mine. "It won't be easy. The age difference, the power dynamic—people will talk."

"Let them." I trail my fingers down his chest, feeling his heartbeat strong and steady beneath my palm. "As long as we know the truth, their opinions don't matter."

"And what is the truth, Lila?" His voice drops.

"That this isn't about designation or convenience or power." I hold his gaze, letting him see everything I'm still learning to put into words. "It's about two people who recognize something in each other. Something rare and worth fighting for."

The kiss he gives me then is like a seal on a promise—tender yet fierce, claiming yet offering.

When we break apart, his expression has cleared, determination replacing doubt.

"Okay," he says simply. "No more hiding. We face it together."

We spend another hour tangled in his sheets, talking strategy between kisses. The Founder's Festival is three days away—the town's biggest annual event, with Nate at its center as mayor. We decide that's when we'll make it clear we're together, not with grand announcements but simply by standing side by side, unashamed and united.

"The committee meeting's at noon," I remind him, reluctantly extracting myself from his arms. "I should go home to change. I can't exactly show up in yesterday's clothes."

He watches me dress, propped against the headboard, something possessive in his gaze that makes heat pool in my belly. "I could get used to watching you in my bedroom."

"You'd better," I toss back, pulling my shirt over my head. "Because I plan on being here often."

The smile he gives me is worth every whisper I'll face when I leave his house.

The committee meeting is held in the community center, where plastic folding tables groan under the weight of festival supplies and planning documents. I arrive early, chin high, prepared for stares and whispers. They come immediately—Councilwoman Doyle's raised eyebrows, Walter's careful avoidance of eye contact, the muted conversations that halt when I enter.

I ignore them all, setting out my notes with steady hands, arranging vendor maps and schedule printouts with meticulous care. Let them watch. Let them wonder. I have nothing to hide.

"Bold move, showing up," Samantha Doyle murmurs, sliding into the seat beside me. "Half the committee was betting you'd quit town by now."

"Sorry to disappoint." I don't look up from my papers. "I never leave a job unfinished."

"The festival, or seducing the mayor?" She delivers the barb with a politician's smile, all teeth and no warmth.

I meet her gaze directly, refusing to flinch. "You know, for a town built on second chances and new beginnings, there's a surprising amount of judgment flying around."

Something flickers in her expression—surprise, perhaps, that I'm not cowering. "This town has traditions, expectations. Nate embodied those."

"No," I correct her gently. "Nate built a place where people could be free from others' expectations. That's what makes Sanctuary special."

Before she can respond, more committee members file in, the buzz of conversation rising as they take their seats. I feel their stares like physical touches, some curious, some disapproving, some openly hostile. But when Nate walks in—crisp suit, confident stride, eyes finding mine immediately—the whispers fade to silence.

He doesn't announce anything. Doesn't make declarations or explanations. He simply runs the meeting with his usual efficiency, treating me with the same professional courtesy he's always shown. But his eyes tell a different story when they meet mine, and the brush of his hand against my shoulder as he passes isn't accidental. Small gestures, easily missed if you weren't looking. But everyone is looking.

By meeting's end, the message is clear. Whatever is between us, it's not a scandal or a secret. It's simply a fact, unannounced but undeniable.

Afterward, as I gather my notes, Marge appears at my elbow. "You've got spine, girl. I like that." She pats my arm with surprising gentleness. "Not everyone's against you, you know. Some of us remember what it's like to find someone who makes you feel alive again."

Her words are a balm I didn't know I needed. As I leave the community center, I spot Deputy Carter leaning against his patrol car. He offers a nod, then something more—an actual smile, small but genuine.

"Festival security plans look solid," he says as I pass. "Good work."

Simple words, but in their acknowledgment of my competence rather than my personal life, I find unexpected support. I'm not just "the omega sleeping with the mayor" to everyone. To some, I'm still Lila Morgan, doing her job well.

Throughout the afternoon, as I check in with vendors and finalize stage schedules, I discover other pockets of acceptance—the florist who squeezes my hand when I place the festival order, the librarian who asks me to join her book club, the barista who refuses payment for my coffee with a conspiratorial wink.

Small gestures, but each one straightens my spine a little more, lifts my chin higher. By evening, as I return to Nate's house—our agreed meeting place now, no more pretense—I feel something like hope blooming beneath my determination.

He's waiting on the porch, whiskey in hand, eyes following my car up the driveway. When I step out, he doesn't move, just watches me approach with an expression that makes my heart stutter in my chest.

"Rough day?" he asks as I climb the steps.

"Educational." I take the glass from his hand, stealing a sip before returning it. "I've learned who my allies are. They're few, but fierce."

His smile is tired but real. "Like you."

I settle beside him on the porch swing, our shoulders touching, a united front against whatever comes next. "Like us."

As night falls over Sanctuary, wrapping the mountains in velvet darkness, I find myself oddly at peace. Tomorrow will bring more whispers, more judgment, more battles to fight. But tonight, I'm exactly where I want to be, with exactly who I want to be with. Everything else is just noise.

11

The morning of Founder's Festival dawns clear and perfect, as if the weather itself approves of what we're about to do. I stand in front of the mirror in Nate's bathroom, smoothing non-existent wrinkles from my sundress, practiced smile wavering at the edges. Today, in front of the entire town, we stop hiding. My stomach twists with nerves, but beneath the anxiety runs a current of fierce pride. Let them stare. Let them whisper. What we have is real, and after today, no one will be able to pretend otherwise.

"You look beautiful." Nate appears in the doorway, already dressed in his mayor's uniform—crisp navy suit, subtle flag pin, the mantle of authority settling on his shoulders like a second skin. His eyes, though, remain entirely personal as they travel over me. "Are you sure about this?"

"Are you?" I counter, turning to face him. "It's your reputation on the line today, not just mine."

He crosses to me, hands settling on my waist, steadying. "I've spent five years being what this town needed. Today I get to be what I want." His fingers tighten slightly. "I want you by my side, Lila. No hiding, no apologies."

I stretch up on tiptoes to kiss him, careful not to smudge my lipstick. "Then let's go face the music."

The town square has transformed overnight into a fairyland of white tents, colorful banners, and twinkling lights strung between trees. My careful planning maps have become reality—vendor stalls arranged in neat rows, children's activities cordoned off safely away from the stage, food trucks parked precisely where we designated. Despite the whispers that have dogged me all week, no one can deny I've done my job well.

People stream into the square from all directions, families with excited children, elderly couples walking arm in arm, teenagers in clusters of nervous energy. The scent of funnel cakes and barbecue fills the air, mingling with the pine-fresh mountain breeze. It should be perfect. Would be perfect, if not for the ripple effect that follows our arrival—conversations faltering, heads turning, whispers rising like disturbed insects.

Nate's hand finds the small of my back, a public gesture that draws even more stares. "Ready?" he murmurs, voice for my ears alone.

"As I'll ever be." I straighten my spine, lift my chin. "You have rounds to make. Go be mayoral. I'll check on the vendors."

He hesitates, clearly reluctant to leave me alone to face the gossip mill. "We're supposed to be doing this together."

"And we will be. For the important part." I give him a gentle push. "Go. The sooner you start glad-handing, the sooner we get to your speech."

As he moves away, greeting constituents with practiced ease, I feel the weight of stares intensify. I focus on my clipboard, on the tasks that still need completion, on anything but the judgment pressing against my skin like humid air before a storm.

"Well, look at you." Marge's voice cuts through my concentration. She stands before me in a floral dress that somehow manages to look both festive and no-nonsense, much like the woman herself. "Head high, shoulders back. That's how you do it."

I manage a small smile. "Trying my best."

"Your best is plenty good enough." She glances around at the festival taking shape. "This is impressive work, girl. Don't let anyone tell you different." Her eyes narrow slightly, tracking something over my shoulder. "And speaking of impressions, you've got company."

I turn to find Samantha Doyle approaching, her festival coordinator badge gleaming importantly on her lapel. Her expression is carefully neutral, but her scent carries notes of displeasure and resignation.

"Morgan." She nods curtly. "The banner at the west entrance is crooked. And we're short two volunteers at the ticket booth."

No mention of my personal life. No sly comments or veiled insults. Just business, delivered in clipped tones that acknowledge my position if not my worth. It's not acceptance, but it's professional respect, however grudging. I'll take it.

"I'll handle it," I assure her, already making notes. "And the sound check for the opening band?"

"Completed fifteen minutes ago. On schedule." She pauses, something almost like approval flickering across her face. "The vendor layout is... working well. Better flow than previous years."

Coming from Samantha, it's practically a standing ovation. I nod, accepting the olive branch for what it is. "Thank you."

As the morning progresses, I throw myself into last-minute adjustments and problem-solving, grateful for the distraction from my nerves. The festival officially opens at noon with the traditional ribbon-cutting—Nate wielding comically large scissors, surrounded by council members and local dignitaries. I watch from the sidelines, clipboard clutched to my chest, simultaneously proud of him and terrified of what comes next.

Deputy Carter materializes beside me as the crowd disperses after the ceremony. "Ms. Morgan," he greets me, eyes scanning the festival with professional assessment. "Everything looks in order."

"Thank you." I follow his gaze, noting his focus on security positions. "Any concerns?"

He shakes his head slightly. "Nothing my team can't handle." A pause, then: "The mayor looks... well. Better than he has in years."

The observation catches me off guard with its simple honesty. Before I can formulate a response, Carter nods once and moves away, back to his duties. But the moment lingers—an acknowledgment, however subtle, that perhaps what exists between Nate and me isn't the scandal everyone assumed.

The hours pass in a blur of activity, the festival hitting its stride as afternoon mellows toward evening. Despite the initial tension, the atmosphere gradually softens as people become absorbed in enjoying the event. I catch glimpses of Nate throughout the day—shaking hands, judging pie contests, listening to constituents with genuine interest. Each time our eyes meet across the crowd, something warm unfurls in my chest, a certainty that grounds me despite the whispers that still follow in my wake.

As sunset approaches, the crowd begins to gather before the main stage for the mayor's traditional Founder's Day address. My heart pounds against my ribs, mouth suddenly dry. This is it. The moment we've planned for, the public acknowledgment we've decided to make.

Nate finds me at the edge of the crowd, hand extended. "It's time," he says quietly. "Still with me?"

I place my hand in his, fingers intertwining. "Always."

We make our way through the crowd, not hiding our joined hands, not flinching from the stares and whispers that follow our progress. When we reach the stage stairs, Nate pauses, bringing my hand to his lips in a gesture too deliberate to be anything but a statement.

"Wait by the side until I signal," he murmurs. "Then join me."

I nod, throat too tight for words, and take my position just offstage as he climbs the steps to the microphone. The crowd hushes, all eyes on their mayor as he surveys them with calm authority.

"Friends, neighbors, visitors," he begins, voice carrying easily across the square. "Welcome to Sanctuary's fifty-third annual Founder's Festival." Applause ripples through the crowd. "Some of you have been coming to this festival your entire lives. Others are experiencing it for the first time. That blend of tradition and fresh perspective is what makes our community special."

He pauses, scanning the faces before him. "Fifteen years ago, when the mining company pulled out, many thought this town would die. That we'd become another forgotten dot on the map, our young people leaving, our businesses closing, our future gone."

The crowd murmurs in remembered concern. I watch from the shadows, heart swelling with pride as he continues.

"But we didn't die. We transformed. We became something new—a haven, a sanctuary for those seeking fresh starts and second chances. We opened our arms to newcomers while honoring our heritage. We built something rare in today's world—a community that values both roots and wings."

His eyes find me in the shadows, something intimate and powerful passing between us despite the hundreds of witnesses.

"Sanctuary was founded on a simple principle: that everyone deserves the chance to begin again. To find acceptance. To build the life they choose, not the one circumstances forced upon them." His voice deepens slightly. "Over the years, I've tried to embody that principle as your mayor. But I haven't always applied it to my personal life."

A ripple of confusion moves through the crowd. This is not the usual festival speech. I take a deep breath, knowing what comes next.

"Five years ago, I lost someone precious to me." Nate's voice remains steady, though I can hear the cost of this public vulnerability. "Many of you knew Rebecca. Knew what she meant to me, to this town. When she died, I buried myself in work, in being what Sanctuary needed. I stopped believing I deserved a second chance at personal happiness."

The crowd has gone utterly still, collectively holding its breath. I can feel the weight of hundreds of eyes, the pressure of expectations and judgments about to be upended.

"Recently, that changed." Nate turns slightly toward where I stand. "Someone reminded me what Sanctuary truly stands for—not just for others, but for all of us." He extends his hand toward me. "Lila, would you join me?"

My legs move automatically, carrying me onto the stage into the harsh spotlight. The crowd's collective intake of breath is audible as I take my place beside Nate, his hand finding mine, fingers intertwining openly.

"Many of you know Lila Morgan as our newest intern, the creative force behind much of today's festival." His thumb strokes across my knuckles, a private comfort in this most public moment. "What you may not know is that she's also reminded me how to live again. How to hope again." He looks directly at me now, the rest of the world falling away. "How to love again."

The word hangs in the air between us—love—neither of us having used it before this moment. My breath catches, eyes widening slightly as I realize he's not just acknowledging our relationship. He's declaring it in the most profound terms.

"I know there's been talk," he continues, turning back to the crowd. "About our age difference, about our working relationship, about what's appropriate." A wry smile touches his lips. "But if Sanctuary truly stands for second chances, then surely that includes the chance to find unexpected happiness, even for your mayor."

For one terrible moment, silence reigns—hundreds of faces staring up at us with expressions ranging from shock to disapproval to something like wonder. Then, from near the back of the crowd, a single pair of hands begins to clap. Marge, her face split in a broad grin. Deputy Carter joins in next, then Walter from the council, then the barista who gave me free coffee, then more and more until the applause swells like a wave, washing away the whispers and judgment of the past week.

Not everyone joins in. I can see pockets of crossed arms and narrowed eyes. But they're outnumbered by the smiles, the nods, the acceptance spreading through the crowd like ripples in a pond.

Nate's arm slides around my waist, anchoring me as the sound washes over us. "Thank you," he says simply, once the applause begins to fade. "For remembering what makes Sanctuary special. Now, let's enjoy the rest of our festival."

As we step down from the stage together, the energy has shifted—not completely, not for everyone, but enough. Enough that when Nate keeps his arm around me as we walk through the crowd, the stares feel more curious than condemning. Enough that when people approach to shake his hand, they include me in their greetings.

"That wasn't exactly what we planned," I murmur as we pause near the lemonade stand, momentarily alone.

Nate's eyes crinkle at the corners, relief and something like joy lighting them from within. "Plans change. Especially when you realize what really matters."

As night falls over Sanctuary and festival lights twinkle against the darkening sky, I stand beside the man who's become my future, watching the town that's become my home gradually adjust to the new reality we've created. It won't be perfect. There will still be whispers, still be judgment. But for now, in this moment, we've carved out a space for our truth—and found, perhaps, more acceptance than either of us dared hope for.

12

—.—

My life fits in the back seat of my Honda. Two suitcases, three boxes, a potted fern that's survived against all odds. It's pathetic and liberating all at once—everything I own ready to be transplanted, like me, into new soil. Nate watches from the porch as I pull into the driveway of what is now our home, his expression caught between joy and terror. I understand. It's one thing to declare your feelings publicly. It's another entirely to clear out drawer space and negotiate bathroom counter territory.

"That's it?" he asks as I pop the trunk, eyeing my meager possessions with something like disbelief.

"Not all of us accumulated furniture-making hobbies and family heirlooms," I tease, hefting a box. "Some of us travel light."

He takes the box from my hands, his own much steadier than I expected. "It's not too late to change your mind, you know."

"About moving in?" The question comes out sharper than I intended.

"About the size of the U-Haul." His smile cracks through the nervousness. "We could get you more stuff. Fill that second closet that's been empty for years."

The casual mention of empty spaces waiting to be filled eases something tight in my chest. He's made room for me—not just in his house, but in the life he's built here. I grab a suitcase, bumping his hip with mine as I pass. "Let's get this inside before you start shopping for me."

The farmhouse looks different in daylight than it did the night I stormed here in anger. Sunlight streams through wide windows, highlighting hardwood floors worn smooth by generations of Carrington feet. The bones of the place are solid, but there's an emptiness to it—a house maintained with care but not truly lived in. Until now.

Nate sets my box on the kitchen counter, hands fidgeting at his sides. "I cleared the dresser in the bedroom. And half the closet. And there's a whole bookshelf in the living room if you need it." He runs a hand through his hair, disrupting its careful styling. "I moved some things to make space in the bathroom too. Not that you need me to tell you that. You've been staying here already. But not permanently. This is different. This is—"

I silence his uncharacteristic rambling with a kiss. "Breathe, Nate. It's just me moving in, not an invasion force."

His hands settle at my waist, grounding himself. "Sorry. It's been a while since I shared space with anyone."

"For me too." I rest my forehead against his. "We'll figure it out together."

Unpacking becomes a strange excavation of my past and his present. Each item I place reveals something of myself: the dog-eared paperbacks that show my love of mystery novels, the mismatched coffee mugs collected from campus events, the framed photo of my college graduation—me alone but smiling. Nate watches each revelation with curious eyes, learning me through my possessions.

In turn, I learn him through what's already here. The kitchen with its professional-grade tools speaks of a man who cooks to nurture himself when no one else will. The living room bookshelves heavy with historical texts and woodworking manuals. The spare bedroom converted to a workshop where half-finished furniture projects wait for completion.

"You can change things," he says, watching me run my fingers along the plain curtains in the living room. "Make it yours too."

The permission unleashes something in both of us. Suddenly we're rearranging furniture, debating paint colors, planning improvements that blend his established life with my fresh perspective. He moves his recliner to accommodate my reading nook by the window. I suggest shelves for his woodworking magazines that have been stacked haphazardly in corners.

"What about this room?" I ask, pausing at a door that's remained closed during my previous stays.

Nate stiffens slightly, hand coming to rest on the doorknob. "Rebecca's study. I haven't… I don't go in here much."

I step back immediately. "We don't have to open it."

He shakes his head, resolution firming his jaw. "No, it's time." The door swings open to reveal a feminine space—floral curtains, a delicate desk, bookshelves filled with medical journals and romance novels in equal measure. A framed medical degree hangs on one wall, dust dulling the glass. "She was a doctor. Pediatrician."

I enter carefully, sensing the sacredness of this preserved space. "It's lovely. She had good taste."

"She would have liked you," he says quietly, surprising me. "Your determination. Your refusal to be what others expect."

The simple statement means more than any passionate declaration could. I place my hand over his where it rests on the doorframe. "Thank you for showing me."

"It can be your office now." He meets my gaze steadily. "If you want it."

The offer takes my breath away—not just space in his home, but in the most carefully preserved sanctuary of his past. "Are you sure?"

"Rebecca built a life here by making this house her own." His voice is rough but certain. "You deserve the same chance."

We don't immediately clear the room. That will come later, when we're both ready. But the door remains open as we continue our tour, a barrier broken, a new possibility acknowledged.

By evening, my clothes hang beside his in the closet, my toothbrush stands next to his in a ceramic holder, and the refrigerator magnet collection I started in college brightens the previously austere kitchen. Small changes that transform a house maintained into a home shared.

"Company's coming," Nate announces as I arrange my books on the empty shelf he promised. "Jake and Olivia. I hope that's okay? They've been asking to meet you properly."

The sheriff and his mate—Nate's closest friends in Sanctuary. I smooth my shirt nervously. "Should I change? Cook something?"

He laughs, the sound filling the room like sunshine. "They're bringing dinner. And they already like you."

"They don't know me."

"They know you make me happy." He pulls me against him, the casual affection still new enough to make my heart stutter. "That's enough for them."

Sheriff Jake Hawkins is nothing like I imagined based on glimpses around town. Out of uniform, he's surprisingly laid-back, with laugh lines around his eyes and an easy smile that transforms his intimidating presence. His mate Olivia is a revelation—a petite omega woman with curly red hair and a no-nonsense attitude that immediately puts me at ease.

"So you're the one who got this stubborn ass to rejoin the land of the living," she says, handing me a casserole dish as she breezes through the front door. "About damn time someone managed it."

"Liv," Jake warns, though his eyes crinkle with amusement. "Let her breathe before you start the inquisition."

Dinner unfolds around Nate's dining table—a piece he made himself, he tells me proudly when I compliment the craftsmanship. Conversation flows easily, punctuated by laughter and the occasional teasing jab between old friends. I watch Nate in this context—relaxed, unguarded, part of a circle that existed long before I arrived—and find myself falling even deeper for this man who contains so many layers.

"You should see the pack runs we used to do," Jake is saying, gesturing with his wine glass.

"Before this one decided being mayor meant no fun allowed."

"I still run," Nate protests. "Just not at midnight after three beers."

"We have monthly pack gatherings up at the lake house," Olivia explains, including me naturally in her invitation. "Next one's a week from Sunday. You both should come."

I look at Nate, silently asking if he wants this, a public outing as a couple.

"We'll be there," he answers, hand finding mine under the table.

After dinner, we move to the porch, the men discussing town business while Olivia pulls me aside, her expression turning serious.

"He was in a bad place for a long time," she says quietly, nodding toward Nate. "After Rebecca, we weren't sure he'd ever come back to himself. The change in him since you arrived." She squeezes my hand. "Thank you for that."

"I didn't do anything special," I protest.

Her knowing smile says she sees right through my modesty. "You saw him. The man, not just the mayor. Do you have any idea how rare that is?"

Later, after our guests have left and night settles over the farmhouse, I stand in the doorway of our bedroom—our bedroom—watching Nate turn down the covers with domestic familiarity. The day's unpacking has left me pleasantly exhausted, muscles aching from carrying boxes and rearranging furniture, but beneath the tiredness runs a current of contentment I've never known before.

"What?" Nate asks, catching me watching him.

"Nothing. Just..." I gesture around us, at the room now containing evidence of both our lives. "This feels right."

He crosses to me, pulling me against his chest, his heartbeat steady beneath my ear. "It does, doesn't it?"

That night, I sleep deeper than I have in years, wrapped in Nate's arms in a bed that now smells of both of us. The house settles around us with creaks and sighs that no longer seem lonely. In the morning, I'll learn which floorboards squeak and how the shower takes a minute to warm up. I'll figure out where the best light falls for reading and how the coffee maker that looks like a science experiment actually works.

Small discoveries that add up to something profound. For the first time in my life, I've found home. Not in a place, but in a person who sees me completely and loves what he sees. As sleep claims me, I send silent thanks to whatever twist of fate brought me to Sanctuary—and to the man who made it live up to its name.

13

A month into living together, and we've fallen into rhythms. Nate rises early, makes coffee strong enough to strip paint, and brings me a mug before I've fully surfaced from sleep. I cook dinner most nights, having discovered a surprising talent for it. Evenings find us on the porch when weather permits, in his study when it doesn't, sharing the day's events in comfortable shorthand. Tonight is no different on the surface—pasta simmering on the stove, wine breathing on the counter, Nate setting the table with the casual domesticity that still makes my heart squeeze. But something hums in the air between us, an undercurrent of anticipation that's been building for days.

I feel it in the way his eyes linger on the exposed skin at my neck. In how my body responds to his proximity, even during mundane activities. In the subtle shifts in our scents, intertwining more completely with each passing day. Nature preparing us for what we both know is coming.

"You're distracted," Nate observes, sliding behind me as I stir the sauce. His hands settle at my waist, thumb stroking the strip of skin where my shirt rides up. "Burn the garlic again?"

I lean back into him, savoring the solid warmth of his chest. "Just thinking."

"Dangerous pastime." His lips find my temple, barely a brush of contact. "Care to share?"

Words tangle in my throat. How do I tell him I'm ready for something we haven't directly discussed? That I want his mark, his bond, a commitment more permanent than shared closet space?

Instead of speaking, I tilt my head, exposing the sensitive juncture where neck meets shoulder—the traditional place for a bonding bite. His breath catches, hands tightening at my waist as understanding dawns.

"Lila." My name emerges rough, almost reverential.

I turn in his arms to face him, needing to see his expression. "I've never been more certain of anything."

Something flares in his eyes—hunger, yes, but also a vulnerability that makes my chest ache. "This isn't something we can undo. Once we're bonded..."

"I know." I cup his face between my palms, feeling the subtle rasp of evening stubble. "I'm choosing you, Nate. Not just for now, but for always. If you want that too."

"Want?" He presses his forehead to mine, eyes closing briefly. "I've wanted it since that first storm. But wanting isn't the same as deserving."

The confession pierces me with its raw honesty. Even now, part of him still believes he doesn't deserve happiness, doesn't deserve me. I press a kiss to the corner of his mouth, gentle but insistent. "Good thing it's my choice too, then. And I think you're exactly what I deserve."

His smile breaks slowly across his face, like sunrise over the mountains. "Dinner's going to get cold."

"I don't care." My fingers find the buttons of his shirt, nerves steadied by certainty. "Some things are more important than food."

He catches my hand, bringing it to his lips. "Not like this. Not rushed between dinner and dishes." His eyes hold mine, serious and intent. "If we're doing this, we're doing it right. Properly. Wait here."

Twenty minutes later, dinner rests forgotten on plates abandoned to the kitchen counter. Nate leads me upstairs by the hand, every step deliberate, giving me time to change my mind. But my resolve only strengthens as we enter our bedroom, now transformed by candlelight he must have prepared earlier, anticipating this moment.

"Oh, Nate," I whisper in awe, taking in the fresh sheets, the candles, the subtle touches that make this ordinary Tuesday evening extraordinary.

He kisses me softly, lovingly. We undress each other with reverent hands, each newly revealed inch of skin christened with touches and whispered words of appreciation. When we finally stand naked before each other, the air charged with promise, Nate surprises me by kneeling.

"I need you to understand what this means," he says, looking up at me from this position of vulnerability, his hands resting lightly on my hips. "When I mark you, when we bond, it won't be about possession. It won't be about claiming or ownership or any of those old-school alpha stereotypes."

My throat tightens with emotion I hadn't expected. Most alphas would never articulate this, would simply take what biology offers without question. "What will it be about, then?"

"Partnership." He presses a kiss to my stomach, so tender it makes my eyes sting. "Choosing each other, every day, even when it's difficult. Building something together that's stronger than either of us alone."

I thread my fingers through his hair, overwhelmed by this man who continues to defy every expectation I ever had of alphas. "That's what I want too."

He rises then, slow and deliberate, his hands spanning my waist as though to anchor me to the world. He lifts me—lifts, not just guides—and lays me across our bed with a gentleness so profound it borders on reverence. The mattress dips beneath my weight, and the hush in the room thickens, pricked only by the staccato beats of my own heart and the huff of Nate's breath as he lowers himself beside me.

His hands touch me—not hungry, not hurried, but with the slow, thoughtful curiosity of a man determined to map a coastline by hand, tracing every indentation and curve and unexpected softness. He begins at my collarbone, his lips pressing a series of impossibly delicate kisses there, working down my shoulder, along the faint line where my skin is lighter from shirtsleeves, over the rise of my breast. His thumbs fan over my ribs, following the sharp inhale I can't suppress when he nuzzles the inside of my arm. I feel like a continent, being discovered for the first time by a careful, awed explorer.

Every touch is a question, every response a wordless answer. He learns them, catalogs them, returns to the places that make me gasp or shiver or melt. The tip of his finger circling my navel. The scrape of his stubble against the sensitive skin beneath my jaw. The way the heat of his palm spreads over my hip, grounding me and setting me alight in the same instant.

He doesn't speak at first, not with words, but with a running monologue of kisses, breathless sighs, the occasional low groan that shivers through his chest and into mine. The reverence in his touch makes me ache—not just below my belly, but in my heart, in the space I had long ago boarded over and labeled private. When he finally lifts his head to look at me, his eyes are glazed with longing, but there's a question inside them, too. *Do you want this? Is this all right?*

All I can do is nod, and then reach for him, pulling him until our bodies are flush. He shucks his shirt, the buttons giving way easily beneath my fingers, and I am momentarily distracted by the span of muscle and scars across his torso—old wounds, healed well, some shallow and some deep, evidence of the life he lived before me, the wars he fought and survived.

He lets me look, lets me trace one pale scar with the nail of my index finger. "That was Jake's dog," he says, and the smile quirks his mouth even as his voice stays hushed. "Wasn't even pissed. Just stupid."

I lean up and kiss the scar, just below his heart, and am rewarded with a breathless sound—half laugh, half moan—that vibrates through him.

When he touches me again, the reverence is still present but now shot through with heat. He slides my leggings down my hips, the cotton pooling at my ankles before being nudged aside. There's nothing underneath, a detail that seems to delight him. He hovers above me, eyes traveling the length of my body, and then his mouth finds the swell of my hipbone, then the inside of my thigh. His hands are everywhere, kneading, coaxing, guiding me to relax, to trust, to open.

And I do, because it's him, because it's Nate.

He moves lower, his breath hot and ragged as he kisses me in the most secret places. I arch against him, helpless under the onslaught of sensation, and he murmurs praise into my skin, words that make no logical sense but feel like truths. *Beautiful. Mine. Good girl, so sweet, so good.*

When he finally enters me, it's a gradual claiming—a slow, deep joining that feels less like sex and more like a wordless oath. He holds himself up above me, watching my face, waiting until I exhale completely before he moves again. And when he does, we rock together in a rhythm so natural, so perfectly matched, that it feels inevitable, fated, like the tide and the moon.

We move together for a long time, slow and bottomless, until my body begins to tremble with the force of what's building inside me. His pace changes, growing more urgent, and his hands grip my hips to steady me, as though afraid I'll fly apart. I feel the distinctive swell of his knot forming, the pressure building between us, and under any other circumstances the anticipation might have frightened me. But here, now, with him, it feels only right—like finally crossing a finish line I never thought I'd reach.

"Look at me," he says, and I do, meeting his eyes as he thrusts into me.

"Tell me you want this," he whispers, the words hot against my skin. "Tell me you're sure."

"I'm sure," I gasp, tilting my head to give him better access. "Mark me, Nate. Make me yours."

The pain—sharp, searing, instantaneous—is somehow a conduit for something infinitely larger. His jaw clamps at the base of my neck, canines sinking deep, right as his body's knot locks us together. The jolt of sensation that shudders through me in that moment is so bright, so shattering, that for a second I am nothing but nerve endings and want. It hurts, and I want more.

My body clenches, every muscle straining for him, welcoming the pain as it warps, mutates, transmutes into pleasure so vast it borders on agony. I gasp, my hands scrabbling at his back, nails raking over old scars and fresh skin alike. He holds me through it—one arm braced beneath my shoulders, the other splayed wide over my belly—every inch of him shuddering as the bond unfurls.

It snaps into place with an audible, psychic click. My mind is flooded, raw and newly exposed. I taste him. The sharp tang of adrenaline, the sweet, yielding ache of surrender, the molten rush of love he's been holding back like a dammed river. His presence expands inside me, prismatic and overwhelming, filling empty spaces I didn't know existed. In a heartbeat, he's there—Nate, not just beside me but within me, our emotions braided together, no longer separate but indivisible.

For a moment, the world narrows to the two of us. The bed, the flickering candles, even the air itself—all of it vanishes under the onslaught of sensation. I feel my own pleasure mirrored in him, amplified, refracted, until it becomes impossible to tell where I end and he begins. I sense his awe, his gratitude, his fierce, protective joy at having me—at being mine, truly and irrevocably. It's so pure it almost makes me weep.

But then another feeling trickles through the bond, something unexpected. A flickering anxiety, a trace of uncertainty that's not my own. I realize, through the haze of aftershocks and bliss, that Nate is waiting—not for my body, but for me. For my answer, my echo, my mark. The bond, while brilliantly alive, is lopsided. The circuit is not yet fully closed.

"My turn," I murmur once the initial wave recedes, nudging him until he understands. With careful movements that don't separate our still-joined bodies, he rolls, bringing me above him, exposing his neck in a gesture of trust no alpha in my former pack would ever have considered.

"Are you sure?" I ask, echoing his earlier question, understanding the significance of what he's offering—equality in what has traditionally been an unbalanced arrangement.

His hand cups my face, thumb brushing my lower lip. "I'm already yours in every way that matters. Make it official."

I lean down, my lips finding the spot on his neck that mirrors where his mark now throbs on mine. I hesitate only a moment before my teeth sink into his flesh, tasting the salt of his skin, the copper tang of blood.

The second connection forms instantly, completing the circuit between us. I feel him everywhere—in my mind, in my body, in the very center of my being. His pleasure crests again, triggering my own, our shared release amplified by the newly formed bond until it's almost too intense to bear.

Afterward, we lie tangled together, my head on his chest, his fingers tracing lazy patterns on my back. The bond hums between us, new and fascinating, occasionally pulsing with echoes of sensation or fragments of thought not quite our own.

"I can feel you," he marvels, voice filled with wonder. "Not just physically. I can feel your contentment. Your happiness."

I stretch against him, cataloging the new awareness that extends beyond my own body. "I can feel you too. It's like... having another sense I never knew existed."

His arms tighten around me, protectiveness and possession tempered by profound respect. "Does it feel confining? Some omegas find the bond restricting at first."

I consider the question seriously, searching within myself for any hint of resistance or regret. Instead, I find only certainty, security, belonging. "Not confining. Grounding. Like I've found my anchor in a world that's always been shifting."

He relaxes beneath me, relief flowing through the bond. "That's how it should feel. Like freedom through connection, not captivity through claim."

We talk softly as twilight deepens outside our window, exploring this new dimension of our relationship through words and touches and the fledgling bond itself. I learn that bonding doesn't mean constant access to each other's thoughts—a relief to both of us—but rather a persistent awareness of wellbeing and proximity, an emotional tether that can strengthen or fade with attention like any other aspect of a relationship.

"We're still individuals," Nate murmurs, fingers combing through my hair. "The bond doesn't change that. It just means we're never truly alone again."

The simple truth of his statement settles into my bones. Never truly alone. After years of isolation—emotional if not physical—the promise of that permanent connection feels like the greatest gift imaginable.

As night fully claims the sky, we remain awake, unwilling to surrender to sleep when each moment of this new awareness feels precious. The bond pulses gently between us, settling into place like roots finding soil, already strengthening with each passing hour.

"I love you," I whisper into the darkness, the words emerging naturally now that our souls have acknowledged what our hearts have known for weeks.

His answer comes not just in words but in a wave of emotion through the bond—fierce protectiveness, profound gratitude, and love so intense it takes my breath away. "And I love you. More than I have words to express."

But he doesn't need words anymore. I can feel the truth of it wrapped around me, inside me, between us in the invisible tether that now binds us beyond anything physical. Whatever comes next—whatever challenges Sanctuary or the wider world might throw at us—we'll face it not just side by side but soul to soul, bound by choice rather than circumstance or biology.

As sleep finally begins to claim us, Nate's arms secure around me and his heartbeat steady beneath my ear, I send a silent message of gratitude to whatever fate or chance brought me to this town, this man, this moment. I came to Sanctuary seeking freedom and found instead something infinitely more precious: a love strong enough to make freedom and belonging one and the same.

14

— · —

Autumn paints Sanctuary in crimson and gold, turning the mountains into a fiery canvas against cobalt skies. The maple outside our bedroom window—I've started thinking of it as ours rather than his—drops leaves that spiral like dancers before settling on the grass. Three months since I arrived in this town with nothing but suitcases and uncertainty. Three months that have transformed me more thoroughly than the seasons have transformed the landscape. I stand at the kitchen window, coffee warming my palms, watching morning mist rise from the valley below our home, and marvel at how completely my life has changed.

Nate's arms slide around me from behind, his chin resting on my shoulder as he joins my contemplation of the view. Our bond hums with contentment, the now-familiar warmth of his emotions brushing against mine like a caress.

"Deep thoughts for seven in the morning," he murmurs, voice still rough with sleep.

I lean back into him, our bodies fitting together with practiced ease. "Just taking inventory. Three months ago, I was running from something. Now I'm running toward something. It's a significant upgrade."

His chuckle vibrates against my back. "Planning to run far?"

"Only to Town Hall. Budget meeting at nine, remember?" I turn in his arms, taking in his rumpled appearance—hair mussed from sleep, stubble shadowing his jaw, eyes soft with affection. My mate. The word still sends a thrill through me, echoed in the bond between us.

"How could I forget?" He steals my coffee cup, taking a sip before returning it. "My mate, the newly appointed Director of Community Outreach, has very important meetings to attend."

The promotion came last week—a position created specifically for me after my successful management of the Founder's Festival and subsequent community initiatives. My own office, a small budget, actual authority to implement the ideas I'd been pitching since I arrived. Sanctuary investing in me as I've invested in it.

"You're just jealous because the council likes my ideas better than yours now," I tease, stretching up to kiss the corner of his mouth.

"Mutiny. In my own town." But his pride pulses through our bond, genuine pleasure in my success that has nothing to do with his position or influence.

This is what surprised me most about bonding with Nate—not the intensity of physical connection or the comfort of emotional awareness, but the complete absence of possessiveness that characterized every alpha-omega relationship I'd witnessed before. He takes genuine joy in my independence, my growth, my ambitions. Supports me not despite my dreams but because of them.

Later, walking through town toward my morning meeting, I'm struck by how differently Sanctuary looks to me now compared to that first uncertain day. What once seemed like a picture-perfect façade now reveals itself as genuine small-town charm, imperfect but earnest. The people who nod greetings as I pass are no longer strangers judging the newcomer, but neighbors with names and stories I've come to know.

Even those who initially disapproved of my relationship with Nate have mostly come around, won over by time and the undeniable evidence of our positive influence on each other. Samantha Doyle still purses her lips when I suggest changes to town traditions, but she listens now before dismissing me. Progress, if incremental.

At Town Hall, I navigate the corridors with confident familiarity, exchanging greetings with colleagues who no longer see me as just "the omega intern" or "the mayor's mate," but as Lila Morgan, competent professional with ideas worth hearing. My new office—once Rebecca's study at home, now transformed into my workspace—displays framed project proposals alongside personal photos, including one from the pack run we attended last month. Nate laughing, arm around my shoulders, surrounded by Jake, Olivia, Marge, and the extended network of friends who've welcomed me into their circle.

The budget meeting runs long, as budget meetings inevitably do. I present my community garden initiative with the confidence that comes from knowing my numbers are solid and my concept sound. When the council votes to approve funding, even Walter—the most traditional of the old guard—offers gruff congratulations.

"Good work, Morgan," he mumbles as we gather our papers. "Your omega house tours idea from last month is bringing in visitors from three counties over. Diner's been full every weekend."

Coming from Walter, it's practically a standing ovation. I accept the compliment with a gracious nod, remembering Nate's advice to let the old guard save face while embracing change at their own pace.

Lunchtime finds me at Marge's, where my usual booth awaits. So much has changed, yet some rituals remain sacred. Marge appears with coffee before I've fully settled, a knowing smile crinkling the corners of her eyes.

"There she is, Sanctuary's rising star." She sets down the mug with a flourish. "Heard the garden got approved. Bout time we had something growing in that empty lot besides weeds and teenage regrets."

I laugh, warmed by her continued support. "Couldn't have done it without your petition signatures. Half the town signed because they're afraid you'll cut off their pie supply."

"Damn right they are." She slides into the booth across from me, a rare break in her usual routine. "You know, when you first walked in here, all big eyes and city posture, I gave you three weeks before you ran back to wherever you came from." Her expression softens. "Never been happier to be wrong."

"I almost did run," I admit, remembering those dark days after the storm, the whispers and judgment that nearly drove me away. "What stopped me was realizing I'd just be trading one prison for another. At least here, the bars were visible. I could confront them."

Marge reaches across the table to pat my hand, the gesture surprisingly maternal. "That's what makes Sanctuary work, honey. Not that we don't have problems—Lord knows we've got plenty—but that we face 'em head-on."

Her words stay with me throughout the afternoon as I finish paperwork and attend committee meetings. By the time I head home in the golden light of late afternoon, I've realized something fundamental about my journey here: it wasn't Sanctuary that saved me. It was the people who refused to let me hide—from them or from myself.

Marge, calling me out on my defenses that first night. Deputy Carter, offering professional respect when gossip would have been easier. Jake and Olivia, welcoming me into their circle without reservation. And Nate, most of all—seeing beneath my carefully constructed shell to the woman who needed to be valued for her mind as much as her designation.

I arrive home to find Nate already there, sleeves rolled up as he prepares for tonight's dinner party. Our first time hosting as a bonded couple, inviting the small circle of friends who've become our chosen family. The house smells of garlic and rosemary, music plays softly from the speakers we installed together, and autumn flowers spill from vases on tables once barren of anything living.

"Need help?" I ask, dropping my bag and kicking off my shoes.

He glances up from chopping vegetables, smile warming his eyes. "Just your company. Tell me about your day."

We work side by side, preparing food and setting the table, sharing the day's events in the shorthand of people who know each other's rhythms. I tell him about the budget approval, he shares news from his meeting with the county supervisor. Simple exchanges that feel profound in their normalcy, their comfortable intimacy.

"You've changed this place," he says suddenly, looking around the kitchen that now boasts colorful dish towels and a spice rack organized by cuisine type. "Not just the house. The town. Me."

I pause in arranging flowers, catching the serious note in his voice. "Good changes, I hope?"

"The best." He steps closer, one hand coming up to brush hair from my face, eyes studying me with an intensity that still makes my heart race after all these months. "You know, before you arrived, this town was running on autopilot. I was running on autopilot. Maintaining without growing. Existing without living."

The vulnerability in his admission touches me deeply. Through our bond, I feel the truth of it—his gratitude, his wonder at the transformation. I lean into his touch, my own emotions flowing freely back to him. "We saved each other, I think."

The doorbell interrupts the moment, announcing our first guests. Soon the house fills with the friends who've become our pack in all but name—Jake and Olivia bearing wine, Deputy

Carter and his beta boyfriend bringing dessert, Marge arriving last with fresh bread and sharp commentary on everyone's choice of attire.

Dinner unfolds with the chaotic warmth of people comfortable enough to talk over each other, to argue politics and tease mercilessly and share food from each other's plates. I watch Nate at the head of the table, laughing more freely than he did when I first met him, the weight of grief and loneliness lifted from his shoulders. He catches me watching and winks, a private acknowledgment that flows through our bond as warmth and belonging.

Later, when dessert has been demolished and conversation moves to the living room, I stand in the doorway for a moment, taking in the scene. Our home, filled with light and laughter. Our friends, sprawled comfortably on furniture we've chosen together. Our life, imperfect but rich with possibility.

I think about the frightened omega who drove into town three months ago, running from a future others had planned for her. How little she knew then about what she was running toward. How surprised she would be to discover that true freedom didn't come from isolation but from choosing the right connections, the right community, the right mate.

Nate appears beside me, drawn by the contemplative mood flowing through our bond. His arm slides around my waist, anchoring me as he has since that first storm brought us together.

"Happy?" he asks quietly, the simple question containing worlds of meaning between us.

I look up at him—this man who has become my partner, my lover, my home—and feel the absolute certainty of my answer resonating through our bond before I speak it aloud.

"More than I knew was possible."

And as autumn wind rustles leaves outside our windows and laughter fills the rooms of our home, I understand at last what Sanctuary truly means. Not a place to hide away from the world, but a foundation strong enough to help you face it. Not an escape from connection, but the freedom to choose which connections matter.

I found my sanctuary in Nate's arms, yes. But also in my own newfound strength, in friends who became family, in a small mountain town that challenged me to become more than I thought possible. In the end, that's the greatest gift Sanctuary offered—not just safety, but the courage to build something worth protecting.

Want more of Lila and Nate's story? Sign up for Ash Jade's newsletter and download a free bonus story!

ALSO BY ASH JADE

Read more from Ash Jade
Short, binge-worthy omegaverse romances where instinct burns hot and love always wins.

Lost Ridge Riders Universe

Welcome to Lost Ridge.
*Where the roads are long, the walls are guarded,
and no omega is ever owned—only chosen.*

Salt and Timber Coast Universe

Welcome to the Salt & Timber Coast.
A rain-bound peninsula where protection is steady, bonds are chosen, and love means staying.

Blackwater Bears

A quiet inland pack where bear shifters offer shelter, endurance, and a home that holds.

The Starfall Ridge Quick Reads Series

Welcome to Starfall Ridge.
Where the crater sparks scents, fate strikes fast, and no one escapes the pull of a mate.

The Yule Curse Series

Four fated nights. Four cursed alphas. One winter where heat burns brighter than fire.

The Touch Her and Die Series

In a world ruled by dominance, instinct, and the pull of fate, every story begins with danger—and ends with devotion.

<u>The Sanctuary Pack Series</u>

Welcome to Sanctuary.
A hidden mountain town where omegas come to heal—and alphas learn what it means to protect.

ABOUT ASH JADE

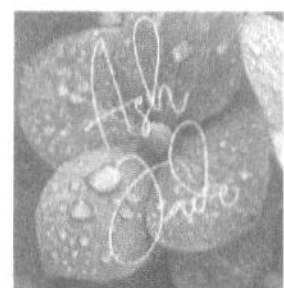

Ash Jade writes trope-packed omegaverse romances full of heat, ruts, and fated mates — but always with heart. Her stories are fast, messy, and addictive, blending primal passion with emotional cores that make the bonds hit even harder. If you love bingeable romances where instinct tangles with feelings (and always ends in happily-ever-after), you've found your pack.

ashjadeauthor.com